INSPECTOR WITHERSPOON ALWAYS TRIUMPHS . . .
H

Even the inspector hims[...] [...] is as ladylike as she is clever. She's Mrs. Jeffries—the determined, delightful detective who stars in this unique Victorian mystery series! Be sure to read them all . . .

The Inspector and Mrs. Jeffries
A doctor is found dead in his own office—and Mrs. Jeffries must scour the premises to find the prescription for murder!

Mrs. Jeffries Dusts for Clues
One case is closed and another is opened when the inspector finds a missing brooch—pinned to a dead woman's gown. But Mrs. Jeffries never cleans a room without dusting under the bed—and never gives up on a case before every loose end is tightly tied . . .

The Ghost and Mrs. Jeffries
Death is unpredictable . . . but the murder of Mrs. Hodges was foreseen at a spooky séance. The practical-minded housekeeper may not be able to see the future—but she can look into the past and put things in order to solve this haunting crime!

Mrs. Jeffries Takes Stock
A businessman has been murdered—and it could be because he cheated his stockholders. The housekeeper's interest is piqued . . . and when it comes to catching killers, the smart money's on Mrs. Jeffries!

Mrs. Jeffries on the Ball
A festive jubilee ball turns into a fatal affair—and Mrs. Jeffries must find the guilty party . . .

Mrs. Jeffries on the Trail
Why was Annie Shields out selling flowers so late on a foggy night? And more importantly, who killed her while she was doing it? It's up to Mrs. Jeffries to sniff out the clues . . .

Mrs. Jeffries Plays the Cook
Mrs. Jeffries finds herself doing double duty: cooking for the inspector's household and trying to cook a killer's goose . . .

MORE MYSTERIES FROM THE
BERKLEY PUBLISHING GROUP...

MRS. JEFFRIES
AND THE MISSING ALIBI

EMILY BRIGHTWELL

BERKLEY PRIME CRIME, NEW YORK

MRS. JEFFRIES AND THE MISSING ALIBI

A Berkley Prime Crime Book / published by arrangement with the author

PRINTING HISTORY
Berkley Prime Crime edition / April 1996

All rights reserved.
Copyright © 1996 by The Berkley Publishing Group.
This book may not be reproduced in whole or in part,
by mimeograph or any other means, without permission.
For information address: The Berkley Publishing Group,
200 Madison Avenue, New York, NY 10016.

The Putnam Berkley World Wide Web site address is
http://www.berkley.com

ISBN: 0-425-15256-1

Berkley Prime Crime Books are published
by The Berkley Publishing Group,
200 Madison Avenue, New York, NY 10016.
The name BERKLEY PRIME CRIME and the BERKLEY PRIME CRIME
design are trademarks belonging to Berkley Publishing Corporation.

PRINTED IN THE UNITED STATES OF AMERICA

10 9 8 7 6 5 4 3 2 1

CHAPTER 1

———◦◦◦◦———

"Poor bloke," muttered George Halisham, the night watch-man. "Twenty-five years married and still waitin' for his old mum to leave off and give up." He snorted as his eyes strained in the feeble light to struggle through the article in *The Times*. He weren't much of a reader, but with there being nothing else to do on these long evenings exceptin' to make his rounds every hour or so, readin' a newspaper was better than sitting here watchin' the wind tinkle the windows on the front of the building. Not that he liked *The Times* all that much, but it was the only one he'd been able to dig out of the rubbish bin when he'd come on duty this evening.

"Not that the old girl'll give up, not bloomin' likely," he said, laughing at his own wit. "Queen Victoria won't give up the throne till she's planted six feet under." He caught himself and glanced down the hallway. There were still lights on in some of the offices. He'd best watch his tongue. People thought you was strange if they come out

1

and caught you talkin' to yourself. He sighed and went back to struggling through the article about the silver wedding anniversary of the prince and princess of Wales. It was either read that or all that rubbish about the death of the German emperor. He didn't much care for the Germans.

A blast of cold March wind slipped in through the crack under the double front doors, fluttering the single light on the far wall and sending chills up George's spine. He glanced up, and through the glass he could see the thick damp yellow fog drifting across the deserted, wet street. Nasty night out, he thought, not fit for man or beast. He went back to his paper, turned the page, and then looked up again. Someone was banging on the front door. Blast.

George put the paper down and sidled out from behind his cozy nest behind the high wooden counter. Peering through the window, he squinted trying to decide if he recognized the man standing on the door stoop. But what with the city being too cheap to keep the one gas lamp outside the building working proper, all he could see was a figure of medium height wearing a bowler hat.

"What be your business?" George called through the glass. He'd been told never to open the doors after business hours. Not since them break-ins last month.

"Open up," the man yelled. "I'm from Scotland Yard."

"What?" The wind blew so loudly he could barely hear the fellow.

"Scotland Yard. The police," the man repeated.

George didn't hesitate. He took out his big brass key ring, unlocked the door and flung it open. "Sorry, sir," he ushered the man inside. "Didn't mean to keep you waitin'. But I'm not to open the doors after business hours. We've had a few break-ins in the past months. Is that what you're here about?''

"That's quite all right," the man said. He wore a large dark overcoat, spectacles, and had a mustache. "No, I'm not here about your break-ins. That's a different department altogether. Is Mr. Hornsley still on the premises?"

George strained to hear the policeman's voice, who was standing quite a distance away and had his head down, almost like he was talking to the floor instead of to George. "There's still a light on in his office," he replied, "and I ain't seen him leave yet. So I reckon he's still hard at it. Works hard, Mr. Hornsley does, sometimes he don't leave until close to midnight."

"Which is his office?" The policeman stepped toward the dimly lit hallway.

"It's the last door at the end of the hall. Come on, I'll show you."

"That won't be necessary. I'm sure I can find my own way."

"No, I've got to announce you. It's the rules, you see."

"Thank you. I'm Inspector Witherspoon from Scotland Yard."

"This way, sir," George shuffled off down the hall. He was dying to know why the inspector was here, but he didn't quite have the nerve to ask. Maybe if he did a bit of chattin'. "Miserable night, isn't it, sir?"

"Quite."

"First the fog," George slowed his steps, "and now all this wind and rain. Not fit for man or beast."

"No, it isn't."

"Must be hard on you fellows, the police, I mean. Goin'

out at all hours of the day and night," George continued gamely. Ruddy hell, if that fellow kept his chin any lower, he was going to trip over it.

"Quite."

George almost gave up. This copper obviously weren't much of a talker. "Odd you comin' 'round at this time of night, sir. Most of the offices close at half past. Course we do get a lot of clerks and such that have to work late. Makes it hard on me, but most everyone is usually gone by now. Exceptin', of course, Mr. Hornsley."

By this time they'd arrived at the door of the offices of Hornsley, Frampton, and Whitelaw, Insurance Brokers. George knew his curiosity wasn't goin' to be satisfied. He'd never get a word out of Mr. Hornsley, either. Hornsley didn't bother speakin' to the likes of George Halisham. "I'd better announce you, sir. Like I said, people is a bit nervous cause of them break-ins."

"As you wish."

"Mr. Hornsley," George banged on the door. "You've a visitor, Mr. Hornsley."

They waited a moment but heard nothing.

The policeman shouldered the watchman aside. "Mr. Hornsley," he yelled, loud enough to make George wince. "I'm Inspector Gerald Witherspoon from Scotland Yard. I must speak with you."

George glanced quickly at the fanlights above the other office doors. He hoped this screamin' policeman didn't disturb anyone else who was working late.

From inside they heard a muffled shout. "Just a moment."

"Scotland Yard," Witherspoon yelled back. "Inspector Witherspoon. Do please open up."

Cor, George thought, glancing anxiously at the fanlights over the other doors again, the bloke's screamin' loud enough to wake the dead. If the other tenants were disturbed, he'd hear about it tomorrow, that was for sure. No matter what happened in the evenings, he always got the blame.

The door opened and a middle-aged man with thinning dark hair glared out at them. "What's this all about?"

"Sorry to disturb you, sir," the policeman said apologetically. "But I must speak with you. It's rather urgent. You could say it was a matter of life or death."

Hornsley opened the door wider and motioned the policeman inside. "Come in then, though I do hope you'll be brief. I'm very busy."

George waited till the door closed behind the two men, debated about the wisdom of trying to eavesdrop, realized it was time to do his rounds, so he grudgingly left.

"Now what's going on?" Hornsley asked, turning and walking toward a patch of light spilling out of an open doorway at the far side of the room.

"This won't take long, sir," the inspector said. Except for the light from Hornsley's office, the place was in darkness. But even in the dimness, he could see four clerk's desks clustered in the center of the room. As one would expect, there were bookcases and file cabinets as well, but they were nothing more than dark shapes against the walls. High-backed straight chairs were strewn willy-nilly between the desks and the walls. The floor was of plain hard wood and he suspected the walls were painted an ugly pale green. Typical London office, he thought. No comfort for the clerks except a meager pay packet at the end of the week. All in all, it looked a miserable place to work. "But we've reason to believe your life is in danger."

"You're joking!" Hornsley turned and stared at him, his eyes widening in surprise.

"We don't jest about murder," Witherspoon replied. He put his hand in his pocket. It was a special pocket, designed to hold a much larger object than usual. His fingers curled around the hard leather at the top. "Perhaps we should go into your office and sit down."

"Yes, yes, of course." Hornsley swiveled about on his heel.

The inspector pulled his hand out of his pocket, tightening his fingers around the end of the instrument he withdrew. He paused a moment, making sure that Hornsley's back was to him. Taking a deep breath, he lunged forward just as he lifted his arm and slammed the heavy object hard against Hornsley's skull.

"Ommm . . ." Hornsley slumped to his knees and fell forward onto his hands, stunned.

From out of his other pocket, the man behind him pulled out a tie. Before Hornsley could come to his senses the inspector stepped beside him, slipped the tie around his neck, crossed the ends and yanked with all his might.

It was over in moments.

The killer knelt beside him, rolled the body over and checked for signs of life. He smiled, satisfied when he realized that Hornsley was dead.

From inside his coat pocket, he pulled out a piece of

paper and a straight pin. He pinned the paper to Hornsley's chest.

Standing up, he listened for a moment. Then he walked to the door of the outer office, cracked it open and peeked out. The night watchman was still gone.

Walking softly he hurried to the front door, checked behind him to make sure that no one was there, and then stepped out into the dark and fog.

Smythe, the coachman for Inspector Gerald Witherspoon, eyed his quarry warily. Betsy, the maid, had her back turned to him and for that he was grateful. He was as nervous as a kitten in a pen full of bulldogs. He took a deep breath and gathered his courage. "Uh, Betsy," he cleared his throat.

She whirled around, her hand still on the bag of flour she'd just put on the cooling pantry shelf. "What? Is tea ready?"

"No, no," he replied. "I was, uh, wonderin' if you liked the Zoological Gardens?"

"The one in Regent's Park?" She smiled. "Who doesn't? They've just added another cat, somethin' called an Eyra. I was plannin' on going to have a look at it sometime soon. Do you want to come with me?"

Smythe stared at her incredulously. Here he'd been screwin' up his courage for the past week to work up the nerve to ask her to go out with him and she done stole his thunder. He wasn't sure if he should be narked or happy. But as he was half-barmy over the lass, he decided not to look a gift horse in the mouth. "That's what I was fixin' to ask you," he said, grinning. "What say we go next Wednesday?"

"Let's see if we can ask Mrs. Jeffries for Monday instead." Betsy shook her head, sending a blonde tendril slipping off her topknot. "It's half price on Mondays, only six pence instead of a whole shilling."

Smythe opened his mouth to argue, to tell her that the cost of admission was the least of his worries, but then he clamped his lips together. No sense in lettin' on about how much money he had. It were a big enough trial to him without Betsy gettin' wind of the fact that he didn't need to be as careful with coin as the rest of the staff.

"Tea's ready," he heard Mrs. Goodge yell from the kitchen.

Betsy, the hem of her blue broadcloth dress swishing prettily, hurried past him and into the kitchen. He shook his head once, called himself a silly git for bein' so bloomin' pleased about their outing, and followed her.

Mrs. Jeffries, the housekeeper, was just sitting down at the head of the table. She looked up, a kind smile on her lips, as the two of them came into the room. Her hair was a deep, rich auburn, prettily streaked with gray at the temples and worn in a loose knot on the top of her head. She had dark brown eyes, a round cheerful face that belied a razor-sharp intelligence, and a short and rather plump stature. Nevertheless, she had the presence of a commanding general when the need arose and when she presided over the evening tea table.

THUMP . . .

Mrs. Goodge, the heavyset gray-haired cook, glared in

the direction of the staircase. "When is that boy goin' to learn how to use those crutches properly?"

THUMP . . .

Betsy giggled, her blue eyes twinkling mischievously. "He's not got the hang of it yet," she said, reaching for a toasted tea cake. "And from the sound of it, I don't think our ears are goin' to get much of a rest for some time to come."

"It's not poor Wiggins's fault he broke his ankle," Smythe said loyally. He was a big, muscular man, with dark hair and harsh features that were softened by a cocky grin and a cheerful disposition.

THUMP . . .

Mrs. Goodge snorted. "Then whose fault is it? He had no business trying to ride one of them contraptions."

"But Mrs. Goodge," Mrs. Jeffries interjected. "Lots of people learn to ride bicycles. It's quite a useful mode of transportation."

"Wiggins weren't no more interested in transport than he is of learnin' to read Latin standin' on his head," the cook declared. "He were just showin' off to that girl."

"Well," Mrs. Jeffries said soothingly. "I expect he's going to be more careful in the future." She peered at the cook curiously. Mrs. Goodge had been in a rather irritable state for some time now. "Is your rheumatism bothering you?" she asked softly.

THUMP . . . THUMP . . . THUMP . . . "Bloomin' Ada," Wiggins screeched in alarm. It sounded like he was bouncing down the last three stairs.

Smythe leapt to his feet. "You all right, lad?"

"Fine," Wiggins yelled back. They heard the bang of

his crutches as he started down the hall toward the kitchen. "Just slipped a bit."

"My rheumatism's fine," Mrs. Goodge said flatly.

"Then is something else bothering you?" Mrs. Jeffries pressed.

She hesitated a moment. "I'm bored. We've not had us a decent murder in weeks. What's wrong with this city?"

"Mrs. Goodge!" Mrs. Jeffries pretended to be shocked. But only because she thought she ought to for appearance's sake. Her conscience insisted she remind the staff that homicide was a terrible and foul crime. They really mustn't wish it upon anyone.

"Oh," said Mrs. Goodge, waving a plump white hand dismissively. "I didn't mean that the way it sounded. But you know what I'm tryin' to say. Life is so much more interesting when we're on a case. I missed the last one, so for me, it's been such a long time."

"I know what you mean," Betsy commiserated with her. "It is right boring when we don't have us a good murder to sink our teeth into."

"If you ask me," Wiggins propped his crutches against his chair and flopped awkwardly into his seat. "I think the inspector's doin' just fine as he is. Do him good to have a rest."

"Where is the inspector this evening?" Smythe put in. "He weren't upstairs in the study when I was up there filling the lamps."

"He went for a walk," Mrs. Jeffries replied.

"The inspector's out on a night like this?" Betsy exclaimed. "But it's right miserable outside." She shivered and ran her hands lightly up and down her crossed arms. "Maybe he's as bored as we are."

"Now we've no reason to be complaining," Mrs. Jeffries said quickly. She wanted to head off another discussion about the lack of murders. "We've had more than our fair share of investigations."

And they had. Inspector Gerald Witherspoon had a phenomenal success as a homicide detective—due, in a large part, to their very secret efforts on his behalf. Not that the dear man had any idea that he was helped by his household staff. Oh no, that would never do. They worked hard, each and every one, to make sure Inspector Witherspoon was completely in the dark about their activities. Of course as a consequence of their actions, they were all now thoroughly bored with the normal household routine. Honestly, Mrs. Jeffries sighed inwardly, she didn't want to have to lecture them. But really, they'd done nothing but moan for days about the lack of murders. Even their dear friends Luty Belle Crookshank and her butler Hatchet had been complaining about it when they'd come round for lunch today.

"Fair share," Mrs. Goodge snorted. "I haven't had my fair share."

"But that's not our fault," Wiggins said doggedly. He was an earnest, kindhearted lad with brown hair and round apple cheeks. "It was your relation that took sick."

Mrs. Goodge had been called away to nurse a sick aunt when they had their last investigation. And she hadn't let any of them forget the fact that she'd missed one.

"We must be patient," Mrs. Jeffries replied, reaching for the big brown tea pot. "I'm sure something will happen soon. Evil sometimes takes a nap, but it never completely disappears.''

"I say, Mrs. Jeffries." Inspector Witherspoon peered over the rim of his spectacles. His eyes were a clear blue-gray, his face all angles and bone, his hair dark brown and thinning. "This is a jolly good breakfast. ''I've not had coddled eggs for ages.''

"Mrs. Goodge thought you deserved something special today, sir,'' Mrs. Jeffries replied. Actually, the cook was still in a testy mood and taking it out on anyone who happened to step into her kitchen. Wiggins was her usual victim, because he, unlike the rest of them, didn't have the good sense to stay out of Mrs. Goodge's way. The only reason the inspector got coddled eggs was because Mrs. Jeffries had cooked them when Mrs. Goodge had gone into the wet larder looking for something to cook for supper.

There was a loud banging on the front door. Mrs. Jeffries put down the toast rack. "Are you expecting someone?'' she asked Witherspoon.

"Not this morning,'' he replied.

Mrs. Jeffries hurried out of the dining room. She flung open the door and found a uniformed policeman standing on the stoop.

"Why, Constable Barnes,'' she said, smiling at the gray-haired craggy-faced man. "What on earth are you doing here?''

"Good morning, Mrs. Jeffries.'' Barnes gave her a weak smile. "Sorry to be callin' so early, but I've got to speak with the inspector. It's rather urgent.''

Urgent? Mrs. Jeffries glanced at Barnes carefully as she

opened the door wider and stepped back. The constable's mouth was bracketed with deep lines and there was an anxious, worried look to his eyes. Something was wrong—very wrong, indeed. "Inspector Witherspoon's having breakfast. Why don't you join him?"

Barnes took off down the hall. Mrs. Jeffries was right on his heels.

"Good morning, Constable," Witherspoon smiled broadly. "I didn't expect to see you this early. I thought we were meeting at the station."

"There's been a change in plans, sir." Barnes took his helmet off and then stared at the tea pot. "May I have a cuppa, sir?"

"Of course. Mrs. Jeffries, do be kind enough to bring the constable a cup." But she was already snatching one from the supply she kept in the sideboard. She watched Barnes out of the corner of her eye as she poured his tea. He was pale, as though he'd had a great shock. Her first instinct was correct. Something was wrong.

"Now," Witherspoon said as soon as the constable sat down with his tea. "What's all this about, then?"

"There's been a murder, sir." Barnes looked down at the tablecloth.

Mrs. Jeffries brightened. Perhaps she'd been mistaken. Perhaps Barnes's demeanor was only because this murder was particularly loathesome. But her spirits sank almost immediately. Barnes hadn't even raised his head to look the inspector in the eye. She poured herself a cup of tea.

"Is that so?" Witherspoon sounded confused, as though he too could sense there was something wrong with the constable.

Barnes cleared his throat. "Well, sir, the chief inspector wants you to report to the Yard right away."

"Constable Barnes." The inspector flung his napkin on the table. "I'm getting the sense that there's something you're not telling me. Is something wrong?"

Barnes nodded. "A businessman named Peter Hornsley was murdered last night in his offices on Lambeth Street. That's one of the tiny little streets over in the City, sir. He was strangled."

"There's nothing particularly odd about that," Witherspoon replied slowly. "People do get murdered, even people in the City. Am I being given the case?"

"No, sir, Inspector Nivens is gettin' it." Barnes's shoulders slumped.

"Then why do I need to go and see the chief inspector?" Mrs. Jeffries wondered the same thing.

"Because, sir," Barnes blurted, "the last person to see Hornsley alive was a policeman. And he called himself Gerald Witherspoon."

The instant the door closed behind the two men, Mrs. Jeffries flew down the stairs. Betsy looked up from the basket of linens she was folding as the housekeeper rushed into the kitchen.

"There's been a murder," Mrs. Jeffries cried.

Mrs. Goodge shoved the sack of sugar she'd just opened to one side. "It's about time."

"Quickly," Mrs. Jeffries said to the maid. "Where is Wiggins?"

"He's upstairs in his room," she replied, kicking the

basket of linens out of her way. "We gave him the brass to polish."

Mrs. Jeffries nodded. With a sprained ankle, the footman wouldn't be much use to them on this case. "Betsy, you must get over to Howard's and get Smythe."

"Should we send for Luty Belle and Hatchet?" Mrs. Goodge asked. "Luty gets put out if she isn't in right from the start."

"Yes, we should. We're going to need all the help we can get on this case."

"Should I go, then," Betsy called over her shoulder as she hurried to the coat tree. "I can pop round there as soon as I've seen Smythe."

"No," the housekeeper shook her head. "We need everyone back here as soon as possible. You get on to Howard's. I'll get one of the street boys to run a message over. Get some tea ready, Mrs. Goodge, we'll have a meeting as soon as everyone is here."

An hour later, Luty Belle Crookshank, accompanied by Hatchet, arrived at Upper Edmonton Gardens. The elderly white-haired American woman was grinning from ear to ear as she hurried into the kitchen. Even Hatchet, her stiff-necked and very formal butler, had the ghost of a smile on his stern face.

"Good morning, everyone," Luty cried. "Looks like we've finally got us a murder."

"Really, madam," Hatchet said primly as he pulled out a chair for his employer, "it's rather unseemly to sound so happy about it. Do keep in mind that some poor soul has been foully deprived of existence."

"Don't take that holier-than-thou tone with me," Luty

snapped. "I heard you chucklin' to yourself when you was gettin' your hat. You've been grinnin' like a grizzly with his paw in a honeypot all the way over here."

"I'm happy about it and I don't mind sayin' so," Mrs. Goodge said. She put a tea tray on the table. "I've felt cheated ever since I missed that last one."

Mrs. Jeffries decided it was pointless to say anything about their attitude. She could hardly blame them for their enthusiasm. After all, it was only natural that people would enjoy what they were naturally good at. And the truth was, they were all born snoops. Even Mrs. Goodge, who rarely left the kitchen, contributed as much as the rest of them. Mind you, the cook did have the most incredible network of sources. Tradesmen, workers, street hawkers, and, even on occasion, some of her old friends. And she pumped them all ruthlessly in her search for clues.

"What's this all about, then?" Luty asked.

"Perhaps we should wait until Betsy and Smythe get back," Mrs. Jeffries said.

"It wouldn't be fair to start without 'em," Wiggins agreed.

They heard the back door open and a moment later, Betsy, her nose in the air, hurried into the kitchen. Smythe was right behind her. "Sorry it took so long," she said, as she took her seat. She shot the coachman a glare. "But Smythe was *busy*, so it took me a while to get his attention."

To Mrs. Jeffries's amazement, the big burly coachman flushed. "If you'da let me know you was standin' there . . ."

"I yelled at you three times," Betsy snapped.

"I didn't 'ear ya, now, did I?"

"Please." Mrs. Jeffries had no idea what was wrong with these two. But the maid was obviously annoyed and Smythe appeared to be irritated and embarrassed. Well, whatever was wrong would just have to wait. They had a murder to solve. "Do sit down and let's get started."

"Who's the victim?" Hatchet asked.

"A man named Peter Hornsley. He was strangled."

"Where?" Mrs. Goodge asked.

"At his office on Lambeth Street. He was a businessman of some kind." Mrs. Jeffries had a bad feeling about this case. A sense of foreboding that she'd never had before. She wanted them out and investigating. "But we've got a problem. Constable Barnes came by this morning to get the inspector."

"So we know for sure he's gettin' the case?" Smythe said hopefully.

"No, he's not getting this one. Inspector Nivens is getting it."

There was a collective groan. None of them liked Nivens.

"Barnes came by because the chief inspector wanted to see Inspector Witherspoon right away," Mrs. Jeffries continued. "It seems that the last person to see the victim alive was a policeman. And he called himself Gerald Witherspoon."

"He never!" Betsy's jaw dropped. "But our inspector weren't out last night."

"He went for a walk," Mrs. Jeffries pointed out. "But as we don't know what time the murder occurred, we've no idea if our inspector was home or not."

Smythe cocked his head to one side and regarded the housekeeper quizzically. "Exactly what are you sayin'?"

"I'm not sure," Mrs. Jeffries replied thoughtfully. "But I have a feeling . . ." She shook herself. No point in getting everyone else all worked up.

Luty's dark eyes narrowed. "What kinda feelin'?"

Mrs. Jeffries forced herself to smile cheerfully. "Don't pay any attention to me. I just think we ought to get started on this case right away. With Nivens in charge, we'll have to work doubly hard to get any information."

Wiggins scratched his chin. "Why didn't our inspector get the case? He's the one that's best at solvin' murders."

"Because he's a suspect," Hatchet said quietly.

"Suspect!" Mrs. Goodge yelped. "But that's the silliest thing I ever heard. Inspector Witherspoon catches killers, he doesn't do it."

Hatchet looked over at Mrs. Jeffries. She was rather relieved to see that she wasn't the only one to see the significance of the situation. "We all know our inspector is innocent," she said reassuringly. "But someone obviously used his name. Let's not jump to any conclusions until we have more facts."

"What information do we have so far?" Smythe asked.

"Just what I've told you," Mrs. Jeffries said. "It's not much, but it's a start. Smythe, can you snoop around on Lambeth Street and see what you can find out?"

"Right." He rose to his feet. "I'll get over there now." He cast a quick, exasperated glance at the maid but she ignored him.

"Betsy," Mrs. Jeffries continued. "I want you to find

out where the victim lived and then get to that neighborhood and start asking questions.''

Betsy nodded.

"How about us?'' Luty asked.

"Find out anything and everything you can about Peter Hornsley. Use your contacts in the City.''

Mrs. Goodge got up. "I'd best get some fresh buns and biscuits made,'' she murmured. "I've got some tradesmen comin' through today and the fishmonger's lad is due to make a delivery. I might as well get me sources workin'.''

"What do you want me and Fred to do?'' Wiggins asked eagerly. Fred, as soon as he heard his name mentioned, raised his head. His brown and black furry tail thumped on the stone floor. His expression was uncannily like the footman's. Both of them looked hopeful.

And both of them were going to be disappointed.

"There isn't anything you can do,'' Mrs. Jeffries said softly. "You can hardly go dashing out and about all over London on crutches.''

"What are you goin' to be doin'?'' Wiggins asked Mrs. Jeffries. "Maybe Fred and I can give ya a hand?''

Chief Inspector Cecil J. Curling was at a loss. He didn't for a moment believe that Inspector Gerald Witherspoon had anything to do with the murder of one Mr. Peter Hornsley. But the situation was decidedly awkward. "Inspector Witherspoon,'' he began, "exactly where were you again last night?''

"Just as I said, sir,'' Witherspoon replied. "I went out for a long walk.''

"I see. Precisely where did you walk?''

The inspector was beginning to feel most uncomfortable. It sounded almost as if Chief Inspector Curling didn't believe him. "I went down Upper Edmonton Gardens to Holland Road, then decided to take a turn around Holland Park."

"And how long did you walk?"

Witherspoon shrugged. "About an hour, I expect. Gracious, sir, you don't believe I had anything to do with this poor Mr. Hornsley's murder, do you?"

"No, no," Curling assured him. But like all good policemen, he was privately reserving judgment. It was difficult to cast Gerald Witherspoon in the role of murderer. But in his twenty years with the police, he'd seen stranger things. "But you do understand why we must ask you to account for your whereabouts."

"Of course, sir."

"And you also understand why this homicide won't be assigned to you," Curling continued.

"Yes, sir." Witherspoon wished his superior would get on with it. He didn't much like answering all these questions, though he could well understand the need for them. For the first time, he understood why people resented being interviewed by the police. It was a most unpleasant feeling. Most unpleasant, indeed.

"And you're absolutely certain you've never heard of the victim, Peter Hornsley?"

"Absolutely, sir. I don't know the man."

Curling nodded. "Very well, Witherspoon, you may go."

The inspector hesitated. "Excuse me, sir. Is Inspector Nivens being given the case?"

"Yes." Curling sighed. He could hardly expect Witherspoon to understand the complexities of office politics or the need to placate those who had friends in high places, those persons like Inspector Nivens. Gerald Witherspoon, for all his brilliance as a homicide detective, was rather innocent of such matters.

Until Witherspoon had begun solving murders two years ago, he'd spent most of his career as a clerk in the Records room. Why, rumor had it that he'd never even made an arrest before solving those horrible Kensington High Street murders. "We're hoping he'll be able to crack this case soon." Privately, Curling thought that the odds of Nivens actually solving this murder were about as good as the prince of Wales sprouting wings and flying to the moon. But, of course, he couldn't express that sentiment. Blast office politics and blast that little weasel Nivens as well.

"Yes, sir, I'm sure Nivens will do an excellent job."

Curling cleared his throat. "The sooner the better, that's what I say. After all," he gave Witherspoon a strained smile, "the killer did use your name to get into the victim's office. We can't have that, now, can we?"

"No, sir," Witherspoon replied glumly. "We certainly can't."

CHAPTER 2

Mrs. Jeffries unrolled the hall rug she'd just brushed and flattened it against the polished floor with the sole of her shoe. She'd spent the morning thinking about what to do and had come to exactly one conclusion: Until she had more information, she couldn't do anything.

Except for Wiggins and Mrs. Goodge, everyone else was out "on the hunt"—and none of them were expected back for the noon meal. She flung open the front door, intending to give the stoop a good sweep. But she stopped, her broom held up in midair, as she spotted the inspector walking slowly down the road toward the house.

She jumped back inside and ran toward the kitchen, pausing only long enough to toss the broom in the small cupboard under the stairs.

"If you don't get out of my way, I'm goin' to wring your neck," she heard Mrs. Goodge shout.

"I was only tryin' to help," Wiggins protested.

Mrs. Jeffries dashed into the kitchen. The cook was glaring at the footman, who was standing hunched over a flattened mound of dough.

Wiggins looked at the housekeeper. "I were just tryin' to give 'er a 'and," he said defensively. "Thought I'd punch the dough a time or two, save her the trouble."

"It weren't ready to be punched, you half-wit," Mrs. Goodge yelped. "And now you've ruined my dough. What am I goin' to do? I've got half my sources due to come through here today! Now, thanks to your 'help,' I'll not have a thing to give them. Unless I give them plenty of tea and some decent bread and buns, they don't hang about long enough for me to learn anything."

"Send Wiggins down to the baker's to buy some buns," Mrs. Jeffries said quickly. "He should be able to manage that, even on crutches."

"The baker's!" The cook was outraged. "I can't feed my sources that rubbish! I've got standards to maintain."

"Well, we'll have to worry about that later." Mrs. Jeffries hurried over to the tea kettle and snatched it up. "The inspector's coming down the road. We must get him a lunch tray ready. Is there any of that beef joint left from last night?"

"Don't worry, I'll get the inspector something." Mrs. Goodge gave Wiggins one more frown and stalked toward the hallway and the cooling larder. "Have it ready in two shakes of a lamb's tail."

Mrs. Jeffries gave the footman a sympathetic smile, put the kettle on to boil, and went upstairs. She met the inspector in the front hall.

"We didn't expect you home for lunch, sir," she said.

"But Mrs. Goodge will have a tray ready in a few moments. Would you like some tea first?"

"I didn't expect to come home, either," Witherspoon replied. His shoulders were slumped and his mouth was set in a flat, glum line. "I think I'd like a sherry."

She hid her surprise. "Go on into the dining room, sir. I'll bring you one right in."

Witherspoon was staring vacantly into space when she came in a few moments later. He gave her a weak smile as she handed him a small glass filled with dark amber liquid. "Gracious, I don't know what you must think, me having a drink in the middle of the day."

"I think you've had a shock, sir," she said sympathetically.

"I certainly have." He took a sip. "It's not everyday that one is questioned about one's whereabouts. I daresay, I can quite understand why some of the people I've had to question quite object to the process."

Her mouth opened in shock. "You were questioned, sir?"

"Yes. It seems the killer used my name. Oh, you already knew that, didn't you?" He looked quite dazed. "Fellow gained entrance not only to the building but to the victim's office by saying he was Inspector Gerald Witherspoon. Oh dear, I'm doing it again. You already knew that too, didn't you? You were in the dining room when Constable Barnes told me this morning."

"I didn't know all of it, sir," she said gently. Poor Inspector Witherspoon, he looked dreadfully confused by everything. "My goodness, sir, how awful this must be for you."

"It gets worse, Mrs. Jeffries," Witherspoon said morosely. "The killer didn't just use my name. He also looked like me, too."

"He looked like you?"

"Yes, the description the night watchman gave when he was questioned fits me perfectly." The inspector drained the last of his drink in one long gulp. "For a moment when I was in the chief inspector's office, I rather had the feeling they thought I might be involved."

"That's ridiculous, sir." Mrs. Jeffries was genuinely alarmed. "Why, you don't even know the victim."

"No, of course not. Never heard of the man until Constable Barnes mentioned him this morning."

She breathed a sigh of relief. She wasn't sure how she would have felt if it had turned out that the inspector did know the victim personally. Not that she would ever believe Gerald Witherspoon capable of murder. But she was very glad the late Peter Hornsley was a complete stranger.

"How was he killed?" She already knew he was strangled, but she wanted the details.

"Strangled." The inspector shook himself again, as though to clear his head of cobwebs. "Coshed on the head first and then strangled with a tie. Oddest thing, Barnes told me he had a note pinned to his chest."

"Was the note pinned there by the killer?"

"We're fairly certain it must have been. Most people don't walk about with a piece of notepaper pinned to their chests."

"What did it say?"

"Nothing that made any sense. It was just letters. V-E-N-I. It could be anything. A name, a place—who knows? Fact is, I won't ever find out. This is Inspector Nivens's case.''

She pursed her lips and looked away so that Witherspoon wouldn't see her expression. Nivens was not only stupid, he was arrogant, suspicious, and petty. Furthermore, Mrs. Jeffries was fairly certain Nivens was on to them. Or, at the very least, suspected that Witherspoon had help with his investigations when he was on a case. Nivens had hinted on more than one occasion that he knew *she* was up to something. They'd have to be doubly careful now.

"But Inspector Nivens has never handled a homicide.''

"Everyone has to start somewhere, Mrs. Jeffries. I'm sure Inspector Nivens will do a fine job. No doubt he'll have the miscreant in hand very quickly.''

Not without a lot of help, Mrs. Jeffries thought. Help that Nivens wouldn't want and would insist he didn't need. "Oh, sir, I'm so sorry. It must have been dreadful for you, being interviewed by your colleagues. What are they going to have you do?''

"I'm going to be working on a robbery case," he shrugged. "I'll get Nivens's case and he'll take this case.''

Mrs. Jeffries was truly alarmed. Inspector Witherspoon had never handled a robbery case. Gracious, they didn't have time to work on two cases simultaneously. But perhaps she was being unfair. There was no reason to believe that her employer would need assistance solving a simple robbery. "What kind of a robbery is it, sir?''

"Jewelry," he replied. "There's a ring of thieves robbing homes over near Regent's Park. You know the sort of thing I mean. They get in quickly while the house is empty, steal whatever jewels they can find lying about the place, and then get out," he explained, trying to make his voice more enthusiastic than he actually felt. The truth was, he didn't know the first thing about catching thieves.

"That should be an interesting change for you, sir," she murmured.

"Yes, they assigned me one of Nivens's best constables to assist me."

"What about Constable Barnes?"

"Oh, they're having him assist Nivens." Witherspoon's brows came together over his spectacles. "But I must say, I do envy Nivens. This case does appear to be most interesting, most interesting, indeed."

"What were you able to find out, sir?" she asked cautiously.

"Officially, nothing. Unofficially, Barnes told me the victim, Peter Hornsley, was one of four partners of the Hornsley, Frampton, and Whitelaw, Insurance Brokers. They're one of the most successful firms in the City. Supposedly they've made pots of money since they started up."

"And when did they start up, as you call it?"

"Oh, the firm's been around for ages," Witherspoon replied. "Three of the four partners went to school together. After they left Oxford, they pooled their resources and opened the company. So I don't think one can look in that direction for the killer."

"What do you mean, sir?"

"I mean that the men have known each other for ages. They're good friends, so I hardly expect one of the remaining two partners is the killer."

Mrs. Jeffries rather thought you could look in any direction for a killer. In her experience, it was often people who'd known you longest and best who wished you dead. But she certainly wasn't going to contradict the inspector in his current depressed mood. "You said there were four partners," she prompted.

"Oh yes, the fourth one recently bought into the business. Some foreign fellow, I believe." He frowned. "Can't remember what Barnes said his name was, but he couldn't be a suspect. He hadn't even met Hornsley. The negotiations were handled by a solicitor."

"How very interesting, sir. I must say, I'm most impressed. But, of course, I shouldn't be. Trust you to find out so much about the case in such a short time."

A genuine smile flitted across his face. "Thank you, Mrs. Jeffries. You're most kind. Naturally, one would be interested in the case. Not that I'm trying to interfere in Inspector Nivens's patch. Oh, no, I'd never do that. But one can't help picking up bits and pieces, can one?"

"Of course not, sir. Did you pick up any other 'bits and pieces,' while you were chatting with Constable Barnes?"

"Not really, just the first names of the partners. There was Hornsley, of course, and Grady Whitelaw and George Frampton. They were the three original partners." He brightened suddenly. "Why, I've just remembered. The fourth partner is named Justin Vincent. Yes, that's right, that's what Barnes said. Vincent is some sort of entrepreneur. Seems to make his living buying into thriving businesses."

"Did Mr. Hornsley have any relations?"

"Oh, yes, he's a married man. I'm not sure if he has any

children. Barnes didn't say. Other than that, I know nothing else.''

"Too bad Constable Barnes didn't tell you what sort of paper the note was written on or what sort of ink was used.''

"I suppose Barnes didn't think it mattered,'' Witherspoon sighed, his sudden buoyancy gone as quickly as it had come. The truth was, though he complained about getting stuck with all the homicides, he really quite enjoyed solving them. Made him feel useful, as though he were truly serving justice. Drat it all, it felt rather miserable not to be investigating this one, he thought.

Even worse, he almost felt as though he were considered a suspect.

"It weren't my fault, I tell you,'' George Halisham moaned. He pounded a fist against the top of the table making his pint of ale shake precariously. He grabbed at it before it spilled over the top of the glass. "How were I to know the bloke weren't really no copper?''

"Corse it weren't yer fault,'' Smythe agreed. "Coulda 'appened to anyone.'' They were seated at a table in the public bar of the Duck and Dog, a pub on the Commercial Docks. Finding the night watchman hadn't been easy; he'd had to cross more than a few palms with silver. But once he'd made Mr. Halisham's acquaintance, he'd had no trouble gettin' the bloke to talk.

"That's what I tried to tell 'em,'' Halisham replied forcefully. "But them toffs never listen to a workin' man. On me all the time, they is. 'Do this, do that, make sure you keep the front door locked, don't be takin' the newspapers out of the rubbish bins.' I tell you, it goes on and on. And now I think I'm goin' to get the sack. Just because Hornsley was done in by some crazy copper.''

''Bloomin' Ada.'' Smythe shook his head sympathetically. ''It ain't fair. But tell me, do you know for sure it were a copper?''

''Nah, it coulda been anybody. But the fellow said he was police, so I let him in. Weren't nuthin' else I could do, now, was there? Besides, with them break-ins we 'ad last month, I thought he were there 'cause of that.''

''You mean the buildin's been robbed?''

Halisham shook his head. ''Nah, just someone breaking in and larkin' about in the offices. Stealin' pens and ink-wells and stuff like that. I don't see why they made such a fuss about it. It's not like whoever done it took anything worth takin', if you get my meanin'. It were a nuisance, nothin' else.'' Halisham broke off and laughed. ''Corse it's nuisance that's done me some good. Them break-ins is why they hired me.''

Smythe didn't see that a few inkpots and some pens being stolen had anything to do with Hornsley's murder, but you never knew. ''What'd the copper look like?'' He took a sip from his tankard of bitter.

''He were a medium-sized like fellow, 'ad on a dark bowler hat and a big overcoat, wore spectacles and 'ad a mustache.''

''What'd his face look like?''

Halisham shrugged. ''Truth is, except for the spectacles and the mustache, I didn't see it all that close. It's right dark in the building that time of night. Mr. Beersch only likes me to keep one light burnin'.''

"How can you be a proper night watchman if they don't let you 'ave decent light?" Smythe said.

"Usually it don't matter," Halisham belched softly. "Most of the offices is empty by the time it gets dark. You don't have a lot of people goin' in and out."

"So it were odd, this Hornsley fellow bein' there?"

"Nah," Halisham said slowly. "Hornsley stayed late lots of times, more than anyone else in the buildin'. That night there were a couple of other firms that had staff workin'. Matter of fact, most of the ground floor offices 'ad someone in 'em."

"So this copper just up and walked into Hornsley's office and done 'im in?"

"I showed 'im in, of course," Halisham corrected. "Walked 'im down the hallway and announced him properly. Not that I needed to, mind you. But rules is rules. Besides, the fellow had a voice loud enough to raise the roof on a cathedral. I'm sure everyone there 'eard 'im shoutin' that he was from the police and 'ad something urgent to tell Mr. Hornsley." Halisham laughed. "Funny that, when he first got there, the bloke spoke so softly I had to strain to 'ear 'im, yet when we got to Hornsley's bleedin' door, he shouted loud enough for the whole street to 'ear 'im."

"Did you see anyone else that night?" Smythe asked.

"No, just the copper."

"Did you see 'im leave, I mean, were he covered in blood and did 'e 'ave a wild murderous look in 'is eyes?"

"I only saw the back of him, he were scarpering out the front door when I got back from checking the rear was locked up proper," Halisham replied. "Fellow were gone by the time I got back to me post. And now Mr. Beersch is talkin' about sackin' me just 'cause I were doin' my job. How was I to know the bloke was murderin' someone? It's not like the copper told me what he was up to, now, was it?''

Smythe clucked his tongue in sympathy. He wasn't just trying to get the man to keep talking, either. He was genuinely concerned about George Halisham losing his position. Life was hard for the poor. Smythe knew that for a fact. He'd been poor most of his own life. Not that he had to worry about that now, but there had been plenty of times when he was younger, before he went out to Australia, that he'd spent more than one night sleeping in the open because he didn't have a roof over his head.

''Corse it ain't your fault, this guv of yours sounds like he's a right old—''

''Right old bastard, that's what 'e is,'' Halisham finished. ''And if I lose me position, I don't know what I'll do. It's not like there's many jobs about, you know.''

''Yeah, I know.'' There never seemed to be enough jobs for everyone. Smythe asked a few more questions, but Halisham could tell him nothing else. He downed the rest of his bitter and tossed some coins on the counter.

''Plannin' on leavin'?'' Halisham asked mournfully. His new friend had been most generous with the drinks and he was a sympathetic sort of fellow too, despite his big, rough looks.

''Gotta get back to the stables,'' Smythe said. ''Look, I work over at Howard's. If ya do lose your position, come by and see me. I may be able to 'elp ya out.''

"Don't know much about 'orses," Halisham said thoughtfully. "But I'm a fast learner."

Smythe reached into his coat pocket and pulled out a guinea. " 'Ere, just in case you get tossed out today, maybe this'll 'elp pay the rent," he handed the coin to the rather astonished-looking Halisham.

George stared at the coin like he was afraid it would disappear, then he looked up at Smythe. "That's right decent of ya. Thanks. If the worst happens, at least this'll keep the landlord from tossin' us into the streets."

"Us workin' men gots to stick together," Smythe said. He nodded to the barman and left.

Outside, he made his way past the stairs of the Dog and Duck, cut through warehouse yards, and skirted wharves until he came to Grove Street. The day had turned dark and cloudy; the dampness from the river seeping deep into his bones. Smythe knew he had no reason to be depressed, but blimey, he was. This morning hadn't gone at all well. Not with Betsy showin' up just as Abigail was throwin' her ruddy arms around his neck to thank him for loanin' her a few bob.

Bloomin' Ada, what rotten luck. Just as he and Betsy was gettin' on so well, too. Wouldn't you know she'd show up at Howard's just at the wrong moment. He'd glanced up to see Betsy standing by the horse stalls with her eyes narrowed and her mouth flattened in a straight line. But what was a bloke supposed to do? Toss Abby into a mound of hay just because she were givin' him a grateful hug?

Frustrated, he kicked an empty coal sack that was lying in the road in front of him. The sack skittered and landed with a thump against the stairs of the Methodist Chapel, earning Smythe a disapproving frown from the well-dressed man coming down those very stairs.

Smythe glared right back. He was in no mood to apologize to a bloomin' Methodist for kickin' a bit of rubbish off the road. His foul mood was all Betsy's fault. The little minx had refused to let him explain that he was just helpin' out an old friend. Corse, he thought, as he dodged round a timber wagon loaded with planks of wood, maybe it was just as well he hadn't explained. Betsy might start wonderin' where he'd got the money to loan Abby in the first place. And he weren't quite ready to tell the lass the truth about his finances. Not yet, anyway. Not till he was sure she cared for him. He had a feelin' Betsy would get right annoyed at the fact that he'd been deceiving all of them from the beginnin'. But what in blazes could he have done? he asked himself peevishly. Euphemia, God rest her soul, had made him promise to stay on and keep an eye on her nephew, Gerald Witherspoon, after she'd left the inspector a moderate fortune and the big house on Upper Edmonton Gardens. Then they'd all come and they'd started investigatin' murders and gettin' to know each other and he hadn't wanted to leave. He hadn't wanted to tell them the truth, either. He was too afraid it would change everything.

He stomped round the corner and stopped in front of the Duke of York Pub. Smythe decided to take a hansom home. Blast a Spaniard, anyway. It weren't his fault he had more money than he knew what to do with.

"Do come in, Inspector Nivens," Mrs. Jeffries said politely. "Inspector Witherspoon is in the drawing room."

"Good day, Mrs. Jeffries," Nivens replied. His dark

blond hair was slicked back, his chest puffed out, and his usually pale, pasty cheeks were flushed with pride.

She forced herself to smile. "It's this way, sir."

"Good afternoon, Nivens," Witherspoon said, as the housekeeper ushered him into the drawing room. "How very good of you to come by. I was going to contact you. I've been given your robbery, it seems."

"Good day, Witherspoon." Nivens sat down on the settee without being asked. Mrs. Jeffries had no excuse to hover; it was too early for tea and she wasn't going to offer it in any case. She nodded to the two men and went out into the hall. Making sure her footsteps were good and loud, she walked quickly down the hallway to the head of the stairs. She stomped down into the kitchen, nodded at Mrs. Goodge, who was serving tea and buns (bakery buns, at that) to a costermonger, and then turned around and went right back up the way she'd come. She took care to be quiet. She crept down the hall and stationed herself to one side of the open double doors leading to the drawing room.

"According to the chief inspector," Nivens said, "you were out walking last night when the murder occurred."

Nivens sounded as pompous as a bishop, Mrs. Jeffries thought. She didn't much like the tone of voice he was using.

"I was," Witherspoon agreed. "Walked for miles. Good for the health, you know."

"Did you know Peter Hornsley?" Nivens continued.

"As I told the chief, I'd never heard of the man until Constable Barnes told me about the murder this morning."

"You're absolutely certain of that?"

Mrs. Jeffries drew in a deep breath. Just who did Nivens think he was talking with—a common criminal?

"Of course I'm certain," Witherspoon replied.

"Do you have any idea why someone would use your name?"

Mrs. Jeffries thought that was an amazingly stupid question. Someone used the inspector's name because it was familiar, since it was in the papers so often, generally after he'd concluded a successful homicide investigation.

"I've no idea." Witherspoon coughed. "Don't you have any suspects yet?"

"Of course we've suspects," Nivens snapped. "But I must ask you these questions."

"Why? I didn't kill the man. Are you sure you've other suspects? I'd be quite happy to help you out in any way I can."

"I don't need your help, Inspector," Nivens replied frostily. "I'll have you know we've already interviewed the victim's brother, Mr. Nyles Hornsley. He's not got much of an alibi and he didn't get along with his brother all that well. Furthermore, there's some evidence the victim and his wife weren't happily married, if you get my meaning. So you can see, I've no shortage of suspects and I certainly don't need any help."

"I didn't mean to insult you," Witherspoon said apologetically. "There's no shame in asking for help, you know. I expect I'll have dozens of questions for you about this robbery I've been given. I've never done a robbery before. By the way, why was Mr. Nyles Hornsley estranged from his brother?"

"Witherspoon, I don't think you ought to be asking the questions here."

Mrs. Jeffries's blood boiled. She could feel the heat of anger all the way up to the roots of her hair.

"Yes, yes, of course. It's none of my affair," Witherspoon replied. "Mind you, if you're having difficulties finding out the cause of estrangement, I've always found that asking the . . ."

"I'm not having difficulties," Nivens shouted. Mrs. Jeffries grinned. "Nyles Hornsley hated his brother because of a woman named Madeline Wynn."

"There, there, Inspector," Witherspoon soothed. "Don't upset yourself. Your face is turning a dreadful shade of red. I don't think that can be good for you."

"Inspector Witherspoon," Nivens said slowly. (Mrs. Jeffries thought it sounded as though his teeth were clenched.) "I think perhaps I'd better be going now. You've obviously nothing further to tell me."

"Oh dear, I was hoping you could give me a few details about this robbery."

"Constable Markham is fully informed about the robberies," Nivens snapped. "He'll give you all the details tomorrow. Good day, sir." He stalked for the door.

Mrs. Jeffries scurried down the hall and whirled around; she pretended to have just come up the back stairs. "Leaving so soon, Inspector?" she called. "Do let me see you to the door."

"That won't be necessary, Mrs. Jeffries," he said coldly. "I can find my own way. Witherspoon's house isn't that big."

* * *

At teatime, everyone, including Luty Belle and Hatchet, assembled around the kitchen table.

"Inspector Witherspoon is upstairs having a lie down," Mrs. Jeffries announced. "So we'd best be careful. We don't want him coming down and accidentally overhearing us."

"I'll keep a look out," Wiggins volunteered. "Fred's gone up with him and I can 'ear 'im comin' a mile away."

"The inspector wouldn't hear nothing important from me," Mrs. Goodge snapped. "I didn't learn hardly anything. Not with someone hangin' about the kitchen and interfering every time one of my sources showed up."

"I was only tryin' to 'elp," Wiggins yelped. "And that's all the thanks I get?"

Mrs. Jeffries inwardly sighed. The cook was notoriously protective of her "sources"; she didn't want anyone else going near them. For that matter, the rest of them were the same way. But she had to do something. Poor Wiggins mustn't be made to feel left out just because he had a broken ankle. On the other hand, she didn't want him possibly ruining a valuable line of inquiry.

"Wiggins," Mrs. Jeffries said gently, "perhaps it would be best if you stayed out of the kitchen."

Wiggins's face fell and she felt like a worm. "Maybe tomorrow," she said quickly, racking her brain to think of something he could do, "you might go out in the gardens and see to it that Fred has some decent exercise."

"You mean keep out of everyone's way," Wiggins said pathetically.

"That's not what I meant at all," Mrs. Jeffries lied. That's precisely what she wanted him to do, because she couldn't for the life of her think of what he could do to help.

"It's all right, Mrs. Jeffries," Wiggins sniffed. "Fred and I'll go out tomorrow and amuse ourselves. Don't worry about us. We'll be fine."

Luty chuckled. "You ought to be on the stage, boy," she said kindly. "Don't fret so. I'll send Essie around tomorrow with a stack of books for you to read. That ought to keep you busy."

Wiggins grinned. "Thanks. I love to read and I've already gone through most of what we 'ave 'ere."

"Now that that's settled," Luty said, "can we get back to business? Hatchet and I had a bit of luck."

"Hold on a minute," Mrs. Goodge interrupted. "I didn't say I hadn't learned anything today." She shot the footman another frown. "Even with him under my feet I did find out a tidbit or two. Seems this Mr. Hornsley was a bit of a womanizer."

Betsy snorted faintly and glanced at the coachman. "Aren't they all?" she muttered.

Smythe's eyes narrowed.

Blast, Mrs. Jeffries thought, seeing the quick look the maid and coachman exchanged, now they're at it, too. But she didn't have time to worry about that now. The inspector might take it into his head to come down to the kitchen any moment now. It was most inconvenient having him home.

"What do you mean?" she asked the cook. "What kind of womanizer?"

"Well, the usual," Mrs. Goodge blushed slightly. "He

was supposedly involved with some woman he kept in a flat in Chelsea. But I couldn't find out her name."

"Is he still involved with her?" Mrs. Jeffries asked.

"No. Supposedly she give him the heave-ho a while back," the cook admitted.

"Can I talk now?" Luty asked archly.

"Oh, sorry," Mrs. Goodge smiled at the American. "Go on."

"Yes, Luty, do go on," urged Mrs. Jeffries.

"Well, Hatchet and I found out that Hornsley's pretty much hated by other insurance brokers."

"Pardon me, madam," Hatchet corrected. "But don't you think that 'hated' is too strong a word? What Mr. Andover said was that Hornsley wasn't well liked."

Luty frowned at her butler. "What he said was that Damon Hilliard had thrown a punch at the man just last week. If that ain't hatred, Hatchet, I don't know what is!"

"Who's Damon Hilliard?" Smythe asked.

"One of Hornsley's business competitors," explained Hatchet. "And Mr. Andover didn't say Hornsley had 'thrown a punch at the man,' he said they'd almost come to fisticuffs."

"Almost come to fisticuffs ain't nuthin' more than a swing that misses," Luty stated. "But let's not argue about it anymore. Andover said that Hornsley's firm was accused of unethical business practices, and this Hilliard fellow claimed Hornsley and his partners were deliberately tryin' to run him out of business."

"By doin' what?"

"The usual—undercuttin' prices, stealin' clients, bribin' clerks for inside information on other firms," Luty replied.

"Did he say anything else?" Mrs. Jeffries asked.

"Not really," she admitted. "But I think that's quite a good start. Nell's bells, this case ain't even twenty-four hours old and we've already got a good suspect."

"Actually, we've got several," Mrs. Jeffries stated. She told them everything she'd picked up from the inspector and, more importantly, from the eavesdropping she'd done on Nivens. "So you see, we have plenty of suspects about. Hilliard, the partners, the victim's wife and brother, and some woman named Madeline Wynn. I think we're off to an excellent start."

"I didn't learn anything at all," Betsy said. "The shop-keepers in the area didn't know Peter Hornsley from Adam."

"Not to worry, Betsy," Mrs. Jeffries said. "You'll have better luck tomorrow."

"Yeah, you'll probably find out all sorts of interestin' bits and pieces tomorrow," Smythe added.

Betsy didn't even look in the coachman's direction.

"Did you have any success?" Mrs. Jeffries asked the coachman.

"Huh?" He drew his gaze away from Betsy's direction and cleared his throat. "Not much. I mean, I didn't learn much more than we already knew. I tracked the night watchman down and took him to a pub down at the docks."

Betsy mumbled something under her breath.

Smythe frowned at her but kept on talking. "Poor bloke is scared he's goin' to lose his position. Seems they're gettin' at 'im for lettin' the killer inside the building."

"But how was he to know?" Wiggins asked. "The killer claimed to be Inspector Witherspoon."

Smythe gave the footman a cynical smile. "The fact the poor fellow was only doin' his job won't matter. They can sack who they like. If they want someone to blame, they always pick on the poor bloke at the bottom of the heap."

"Is this Mr. Halisham certain that no one else came into the building other than the man calling himself Inspector Witherspoon?" Mrs. Jeffries asked.

"Positive," Smythe stated. "Halisham come back from checking the back door just in time to see the false Witherspoon lettin' 'imself out the front door. He shouted 'good night' at 'im, but the man was out the door by then and didn't answer. Halisham went right up to double-check that the front door lock had clicked into place. No one else came in."

"Did Halisham give you a description of the man calling himself Inspector Witherspoon?" Luty asked eagerly. "I mean, what did this feller look like?"

"Accordin' to what Halisham saw, he fits our inspector right down to 'is bowler 'at and 'is spectacles. Mind you, Halisham did say there were only one light. He didn't really get a good look at the man's face. Corse he never thought the man weren't really with Scotland Yard, not with 'im bellowin' out who he was and who he wanted to see all the way down the 'all to Hornsley's office. Halisham told me 'e were worried someone would stick their 'ead out just to see what were goin' on. There was others workin' late that night." He went on to give them the rest of the details he'd learned from the watchman.

When he finished, Hatchet leaned forward on his elbows. "Did anyone else go out?"

"Only the few people that was workin' on the ground

floor," Smythe said. "There was a clerk working in the architect's office and he left at seven o'clock. The estate agent, he was workin' late, too; he left at around half-past seven."

"What time was the body found?" Mrs. Goodge asked.

"Round ten last night," Smythe explained.

"By whom?" Wiggins asked.

"Halisham. When it got late and Hornsley hadn't come out of his office, Halisham got curious," Smythe explained. "He knocked on the door and the ruddy thing swung open. He said it were a bit dark, the only light was from one of the inner offices, but he said he could see Hornsley there layin' on the floor. He thought the man had had a fit or something. But when he got close, he could tell the man was dead. So he ran for the copper on the corner."

"Was anything missing?" Betsy finally asked. "I mean, could it have been a robbery?"

"Halisham overheard one of the other partners, fellow named Frampton, talkin' to the police this morning. Accordin' to Frampton, nothing was missin'." Smythe tried a smile. Betsy stared at him stone-faced. "Anyways," he continued, "the firm didn't keep cash or valuables on the premises."

"Excellent, Smythe," Mrs. Jeffries said kindly. She felt rather sorry for the poor man. Obviously Betsy was furious at him and, just as obviously, he hadn't a clue what to do about it. She asked if anyone else had anything to report, but no one did.

"Before we continue," Mrs. Jeffries said, "a word of warning. Inspector Nivens is handling this case and he'll be on the lookout for any of us sneaking about and asking questions. We must be very, very careful. Is that understood?''

"Course it is." Luty thumped her cane on the floor. "We all knows this Nivens is a sneaky little varmint, so I reckon we'll all keep our eyes open."

"For once, madam," Hatchet said, "I agree with you."

For the next ten minutes they discussed what to do next. As soon as everyone had their assignments, Luty and Hatchet took their leave. Mrs. Jeffries, Mrs. Goodge, and Betsy tidied up the kitchen and Smythe took Fred, who'd sneaked downstairs as soon as the inspector had gone to sleep, out for a walk.

Smythe thought his luck had changed when he came back into the kitchen and saw Betsy putting the last of the china in the cupboard. There was no sign of the cook or the housekeeper and Wiggins had hobbled up to his room earlier. Smythe cleared his throat. He saw Betsy's back stiffen but she didn't turn around and acknowledge his presence. "Uh, Betsy, could I have a word, please?"

"What about?"

"About this morning at the stables," he said. Blast! Who'd have thought his past would surface now to come back and haunt him. "I'd like to explain somethin' to you."

"You've nothing to explain," she said. She turned to face him, her chin was raised and her blue eyes glinted with anger. "It's nothing to me what you do or who you spend your time with. If you want to be givin' women money . . ."

Blast and damn, he thought. She'd seen him giving Abigail a wad of pound notes.

"It's none of my business."

"True," he said bluntly. Frankly, it weren't none of her concern. Exceptin' that he cared about her, cared more than he'd ever thought it possible to care about anyone. "But yer my friend and I won't 'ave you thinkin' badly of me. I was givin' that woman money 'cause she's an old friend of mine and she's a bit down on her luck, that's all."

Betsy stared at him poker-faced. He was sure she didn't believe a word he'd said.

CHAPTER 3

———❧———

"Haven't you finished yet?" Mrs. Goodge pointed to Smythe's plate. "You've been playing with that sausage for the past ten minutes. And you, Wiggins, are you goin' to eat that egg or not?"

"What's the ruddy 'urry?" Smythe replied. He wasn't in the best of moods himself. Betsy was still acting like she had a poker up her spine and he hadn't slept all that well for worrying about it. "We only just set down a few minutes ago."

Mrs. Jeffries glanced at the clock. It had barely gone half-past seven. "We've plenty of time to enjoy our breakfast, Mrs. Goodge," she said. "It's still very early. The inspector won't be wanting his breakfast for another half hour."

Betsy reached for another piece of toast. "You've been rushin' us ever since we come down," she complained. "What's got into you this morning? Your rheumatism actin' up again?"

The cook put her hands on her ample hips and frowned. "There's nothing wrong exceptin' that I need to get this kitchen cleared. I've got my cousin Hilda's boy comin' by early and I want to have plenty of time to talk to the lad. He works as footman for a family that lives round the corner from Peter Hornsley."

"What time is he due?" Mrs. Jeffries asked patiently.

"Half-past eight," she replied, hurrying over to the oven and opening the door. "But I want to get some things done before he gets here. He's not the only one coming by today."

"I suppose all of us have a lot to do today," Mrs. Jeffries said as she reached for the marmalade.

"I don't," Wiggins complained. "Me and Fred 'as got nuthin' to do but 'ang about 'ere polishin' the ruddy silver."

"Not to worry, lad," Smythe said kindly. "The rest will do you good. But mind you stay out of Mrs. Goodge's way."

"Luty said she was sendin' Essie over with some books for you to read," Betsy added. "That ought to help keep you occupied."

"Yeah, but Essie'll 'ang about for ages," Wiggins groaned. "I'll never get rid of 'er."

"The lass likes ya," Smythe teased.

Wiggins blushed. Essie was a girl that Luty had taken in after she'd lost her position as a maid. They'd met the girl when they were investigating one of their first cases. Oddly enough, Hatchet had taken the girl under his wing, taught her to read, and there was now talk of sending her off to school somewhere. But that didn't make her any prettier,

Wiggins thought peevishly. Truth to tell, she was homely. He winced guiltily, wondering if the others could see what he was thinking. He really should be ashamed of himself; Essie was a right nice girl. And smart, too, despite the fact that she had teeth that stuck out funny.

"As we're all getting a fairly early start today," Mrs. Jeffries said, "why don't we meet back here at noon?"

Betsy frowned. "I don't know. I'm not sure that'll give me enough time. I wanted to talk to the shopkeepers 'round the Hornsley neighborhood and then I wanted to have a go at making contact with someone from the household."

"After I do the pubs," Smythe added, "I wanted to talk to the cabbies in the area. You never know what you might stumble across if you get lucky. I'd not like to have to 'urry back just when I've got someone talkin'."

Mrs. Jeffries gazed at them thoughtfully. She was really quite proud. They did take their detecting very seriously. "You're right. I suppose it's not a good idea to meet here so early. Why don't we meet for an early tea before supper?"

"That would be easier on me," the cook said quickly. "That way I wouldn't have to worry about fixing a noon meal."

"What are you goin' to be doin' today?" Wiggins asked Mrs. Jeffries. "Maybe I could 'elp you?"

"I'm sorry, Wiggins," the housekeeper smiled sympathetically. "But I'm meeting Dr. Bosworth."

"Oh, no," Betsy cried. "You're not!"

Surprised, Mrs. Jeffries stared at the maid. "Why shouldn't I see Dr. Bosworth? With any luck, he'll have done the postmortem on Hornsley. He might have some valuable information to tell us.''

''But you said we had to be careful,'' Betsy argued. ''What if Dr. Bosworth mentions you were snoopin' about?''

''The lass 'as got a point,'' Smythe interjected. ''We've got to be right cautious on this case. It's not even the inspector's.''

Mrs. Jeffries frowned thoughtfully. They did have a point. ''But I've used . . .'' She broke off, appalled at herself for saying such a thing. ''I mean,'' she amended, ''we've had help from Dr. Bosworth several times before. I'm sure he's absolutely trustworthy. Besides, I'll make sure and tell him to keep my inquiries confidential.''

''Hello, hello,'' the voice of Lady Cannonberry came from the back hallway. ''Anyone home?''

''We're in here,'' Mrs. Jeffries called.

''Oh, dear,'' said Ruth Cannonberry, an attractive middle-aged woman, who blushed to the roots of her blonde hair when she saw she'd interrupted their breakfast. ''I'm so sorry. I shouldn't have barged in as I did.''

''Rest assured,'' Mrs. Jeffries said politely, ''you're most welcome at any time. May we offer you some breakfast?''

''I've eaten, thank you.'' Ruth took a seat beside Wiggins. She reached down and patted Fred on the head. ''But I could do with a cup of tea.''

''I'll get the cup,'' Betsy said, getting up and going to the cupboard.

''I've missed seeing any of you about the gardens the last day or two. Thank you, Betsy,'' she said as the maid set the cup in front of her. "So naturally I thought you must be investigating this dreadful murder."

"What murder?" Mrs. Jeffries tried to keep her tone as neutral as possible. Blast. How on earth had she found out?

"Why, the one Wiggins told me about yesterday afternoon." Ruth smiled at the footman. Wiggins's round cheeks turned red and he slumped down in his seat as all eyes turned on him.

"Oh, that murder," Mrs. Goodge muttered. She shot the footman a glare that would have singed the blackening off an oven.

"I must say I think it's dreadfully unfair of Scotland Yard to suspect Inspector Witherspoon," Ruth continued.

"I suppose Wiggins told you that, too," Betsy said.

"Inspector Witherspoon is not a suspect," Mrs. Jeffries said firmly. "But because the murderer used his name to get into the victim's office, naturally, he can't investigate the case."

"Does that mean you're not investigating it?" Ruth asked.

"Well," Mrs. Jeffries would have straight out lied to her guest, but she was fairly sure she'd get caught. All anyone had to do was watch the household and they could see if they were on a case or not. "Actually, we are investigating this one."

"Oh, goody," Ruth clapped her hands together. "I'm so very glad. I was terrified you were going to pass this one up. Now, what can I do to help?"

Constable Barnes felt like a traitor. But duty was duty and he'd been temporarily assigned to assist Inspector Nivens.

Translated, that meant the brass was afraid of a right old muck up and they wanted him on the scene to keep Nivens from doing too much damage.

"Do stand still, Constable," Nivens snapped. "We're here to ask questions, not to memorize the paintings on Mrs. Hornsley's wall."

"Sorry, sir," Barnes apologized. He drew his gaze away from the pretty oil of a pastoral English meadow. What was he supposed to look at, he wondered, the furniture?

He glanced about the drawing room. There was a marble fireplace on one side, two wide double windows on the wall facing the garden, a thick red and gold fleur-de-lis patterned carpet, and a number of balloon-backed chairs and settees. It was a nice room, elegant and beautifully but unimaginatively decorated. There was cream-colored paint on the walls and bronze velvet drapes framing the windows, fringed shawls on the tables, and several nice pieces of china and silver knicknacks scattered about, but blimey, there wasn't much to keep a man's mind occupied.

Finished with his examination of the Hornsley drawing room, Barnes gave Nivens a quick frown. Not stare at paintings? Wasn't that what they was there for? To be looked at? Nivens was a ruddy fool.

Nivens straightened as they heard footsteps coming down the hall. A tall, slender middle-aged woman with dark brown hair and blue eyes swept into the room. She was dressed in heavy black mourning clothes that rustled softly as she came toward the two policemen.

Her face was pale, and her lips were bloodless, as though she'd recently been ill. She'd once been a handsome woman, but now there were deeply bracketed age lines etched around her eyes and mouth.

"Mrs. Hornsley," Nivens stepped forward and gave a slight bow. "Do forgive us for intruding at a time like this, but, unfortunately, there are some questions that must be asked."

"And you are?" Glynis Hornsley stared at him blankly.

"Inspector Nigel Nivens," he clicked his heels together. "Scotland Yard. We're here to ask you a few questions about your late husband."

Barnes frowned. Inspector Witherspoon didn't do them poncy little bows or that silly heel clickin'. Who did Nivens think he was—one of the Kaiser's generals?

Glynis Hornsley nodded. "Yes, I thought you might be coming round. I just didn't expect it so soon. Peter isn't even buried yet."

"We have to do the postmortem on your husband," Barnes said gently. "That delays things a bit."

Nivens frowned irritably at the constable. Then he looked pointedly at the settee, but as Mrs. Hornsley was still standing, he could hardly sit down himself. Barnes stifled a grin.

"Mrs. Hornsley," Nivens began, "what time was your husband due to come home last night?"

"I don't know," she replied. "He'd been very busy lately and had been working later and later hours."

"So he didn't tell you what time to expect him?"

"No, he merely asked for the cook to keep something hot for his dinner and that he'd be home sometime in the evening."

"I see," Nivens said.

Barnes couldn't figure out what Nivens had seen; all

they'd learned was that the man was a hard worker and had been puttin' in a lot of long hours at his office. But as they'd already learned that same information from one of Hornsley's partners, he didn't see why Nivens was wasting time covering the same ground.

"Were you here all evening?" Nivens asked.

Good, thought Barnes, now he's starting to ask some decent questions.

"Yes, I was. I rarely go out in the evenings." She shrugged. "Peter isn't very sociable. I've learned to entertain myself, Inspector. I read a great deal."

"Did your husband have any enemies?" Nivens asked.

"Of course he did," Mrs. Hornsley said. "He wasn't a particularly agreeable man. There were people in London that loathed him."

"Who?"

"I can't give you names," she said tartly. "Peter didn't confide his business troubles to me. But I know that some of his competitors hated him."

"Enough to murder him?" Nivens prodded.

Barnes felt like shaking the man. For God's sake, there were a dozen or more things he should be askin'. What was wrong with the man? Why wasn't he askin' if someone could confirm her whereabouts last night? Why wasn't he asking *who* was goin' to benefit from Hornsley's death? They already knew that Hornsley's competitors hated him. They'd gotten that information this morning from his nervous Nellie of a partner, Grady Whitelaw.

"I don't know about that." Glynis Hornsley shrugged. "I'm sorry, I know I'm not being very helpful, but this has been a dreadful shock to me."

"Yes, we can appreciate that," Nivens said. "Had your husband received any threats to his life?"

"No, not that I know of."

"Are you sure, Mrs. Hornsley?" Nivens pressed. "Perhaps a staff person he'd sacked, a business rival he'd angered? Anything like that."

"Inspector, he's received nothing that I know about in the way of threats," she said tersely. "As for former staff members, Peter frequently sacked people. He rather enjoyed doing it. But none of them ever threatened him. My husband," her mouth curled in a sneer as she spoke, "always took great pains to bully those who weren't able or likely to fight back. He was quite good at picking his victims, you see. He's been doing it all his life."

"So you've no idea who would have wanted to harm your husband?" Nivens didn't react at all to the woman's tone or words. Barnes wondered if they had even registered on the man.

"All I can think is that it's probably some business rival," she answered.

Ask her about the note, Barnes silently screamed at Nivens. Ask her about the writing on the ruddy note. Ask her if she's any idea what VENI might mean.

"Yes, that's our view as well," Nivens agreed. "Well, we shan't bother you further." He bowed again. "My deepest condolences for your loss."

Barnes could have spit. How the bloomin' blue blazes could Nivens have formed any kind of an opinion? He'd not asked enough questions to know anything, let alone that Hornsley was killed by a business rival.

There were plenty of businessmen in the City, and as

far as Barnes knew, most of them didn't get rid of their competition by chokin' them to death. Furthermore, all you had to do was spend two minutes with the grieving widow and it was as plain as the nose on your face that she hated her husband and wasn't terribly sorry he was dead.

"Is this the street, then?" Smythe asked.

"Hornsley's house is the last one at the end," Betsy replied. She pointed down the row of large Georgian homes on the quiet street. "But I think I'll nip back up the High Street and see what I can get out of the shopkeepers."

"No hansoms that I can see," Smythe muttered. The neighborhood was quiet, elegant, and without the clamor of street traffic. "So maybe I'll try that pub we passed on the corner. Uh, Betsy, what time you figurin' on goin' back?"

"I don't know," she replied, looking everywhere but directly at him. "When I get finished, I suppose."

Smythe felt like he was talking to a stranger. All the way over here, Betsy had been so polite you'd have thought he was the ruddy prince of Wales. What did the girl want? He'd told her the truth, told her that Abigail was just an old friend. But she was actin' like she'd caught him kissin' a floozie under the stairs. Women! Who could understand 'em?

He gathered his courage and made one more stab at it. "Do you want me to 'ang about until you get through?" he asked, trying hard to keep his tone casual and matter-of-fact.

Betsy lifted her chin slightly. "I can find my own way

home. You don't have to wait for me. I wouldn't want to put you to any trouble, not on my account.''

"I know I don't '*ave* to do it," he shot back, starting to get really narked by her attitude. "But I thought it would be polite to offer seein' as 'ow we're both 'ere."

"Don't bother." She shrugged.

"All right, then," he snapped. "I'll be off to the pubs. See you this evenin'."

"Fine." She retorted, giving him a quick look. "I wouldn't want to drag you away from the pubs. Maybe your 'old friend' will show up."

With that, she turned and marched down the street, leaving Smythe to glare helplessly at her back.

Constable Barnes's mood didn't improve when he accompanied Inspector Nivens back to the offices of Hornsley, Frampton, and Whitelaw. He'd not sat down all morning, his feet hurt, he wanted a cup of tea, and though he'd been taught to respect his superiors, he couldn't stick Nivens.

The man had finished questioning Mrs. Hornsley and then hadn't even asked to speak to the servants. How would they ever find out anything about Glynis Hornsley!

She claimed she'd been home during the time of the murder, but ruddy hell, Nivens hadn't even had the brains to confirm that with the housekeeper. But when Barnes had gently suggested they question the staff to learn more about Mrs. Hornsley, Nivens had sneered at him. Told him that they already knew the killer was a man, and did Constable Barnes think that Mrs. Hornsley had put on a false mustache and gone out to strangle her husband?

Stupid fool. Nivens had been a copper long enough to

know the basics. Hadn't the man ever heard of murder for hire?

Inspector Witherspoon wouldn't have made a mistake like that! He'd have questioned everyone.

It was that kind of attention to detail that made Witherspoon the genius he was at solving crimes. One little word spoken by a housemaid, one clue discovered by an unexpected question, and Bob's your uncle. Inspector Witherspoon would find that last piece of the puzzle and before you could snap your fingers, the killer would be facing a judge and jury.

Barnes glanced at Nivens, who was pacing importantly up and down the room of the outer office, his chest puffed out and his hands thrust into his pockets. The constable snorted softly. Silly git. At the rate they were going, Barnes would be ready to retire before they found this killer.

The door to one of the inner offices opened and a clerk stepped out. "Mr. Frampton will see you now," he said to Nivens.

Nivens and Barnes followed the clerk into the office. George Frampton, a middle-aged portly man with close-cropped blond hair, muttonchop whiskers, and spectacles, rose from behind a desk.

"I'm sorry to keep you waiting, Inspector," he said. "Please sit down." He gestured toward the one chair in front of the desk.

"Thank you." Nivens sat. "We're here to ask you a few questions about Peter Hornsley's death. We spoke with Mr. Whitelaw earlier today."

"Have you made any progress in finding the murderer?" Frampton asked. He drummed his fingers on the top of an open ledger. "I must admit, the whole thing has affected me terribly. Dreadful business, absolutely dreadful."

"Murder always is," Nivens replied. "Mr. Frampton, Mrs. Hornsley seems to think the killer was probably a business rival of Hornsley's."

Frampton's eyebrows rose. "Really?"

"You don't think that's possible?"

"I suppose it's possible," Frampton said slowly. He picked up a pen and began twitching it from side to side. "But I don't believe our firm has any more enemies than any other business. That's hardly an acceptable way of dealing with one's competitors."

At least this one wasn't a complete idiot, Barnes thought.

"But then again," Frampton continued, "one never knows."

"Can you think of anyone who would have wanted Mr. Hornsley dead?"

Frampton shrugged. "No."

Barnes cleared his throat. "Excuse me, sir," he said to Nivens. "But I think I ought to question the clerks, with Mr. Frampton's permission, of course."

Nivens gave him a cold, fishlike stare, but as the constable was only doing his proper job, he couldn't find any grounds for refusing the request. "All right, Barnes," he looked at Frampton. The man nodded. "But mind you don't upset the routine," Nivens warned as Barnes escaped for the door.

Upset the routine, Barnes snorted again. There'd been a bloomin' murder committed, wasn't that enough to upset the routine! He wondered how Nivens had ever made it into the detective ranks.

The clerk who'd shown them into the office was sitting at the desk closest to Frampton's door. "Excuse me," Barnes said, "but I'd like to ask you a few questions. What's your name?"

"Hammer, sir. Jonathan Hammer." He pushed a stack of papers to one side. "But I don't know what I can tell you. I'd already gone home when Mr. Hornsley was killed."

"How long have you worked here?" Barnes asked.

"Five years, sir."

"And on the day of the murder, what time did you leave?" Barnes noticed the other two clerks had given up all pretense of working and were openly eavesdropping.

"I left at half-past five, sir," Hammer said. "With all the others. The only person left in the office was Mr. Hornsley."

"Why was Mr. Hornsley working late?"

Hammer shrugged. "I'm not sure, sir. I expect it had something to do with work. But he weren't one to explain his actions to a clerk."

Barnes nodded. "Do you know if Mr. Hornsley had any enemies?" Ye Gods, he thought, as soon as the sentence had left his mouth. Now he was doing it. Of course Hornsley had enemies, someone had strangled him.

"Well," Hammer glanced at Frampton's door. "Some of our competitors didn't like him all that much."

"Tell him about Hilliard," another clerk hissed. "Tell him what happened last week."

"Hilliard," Barnes prompted. "Who's he?"

"He owns a rival firm," Hammer explained, his voice rising in excitement. "And he come here last week and accused Mr. Hornsley of trying to run him out of business. Claimed Mr. Hornsley had bribed one of his clerks for information and undercut his rate.''

''Had Mr. Hornsley done that?''

Hammer glanced uneasily toward Frampton's closed door. ''I don't rightly know. But I think it's likely.''

''Is that all?'' Barnes prompted.

''Tell him about the set-to here in the office,'' the other clerk encouraged. ''Go on, tell him.''

Barnes waited. Hammer gave the closed door another worried glance and then leaned toward the constable. ''Mr. Hilliard come in here last week. He and Mr. Frampton went into Mr. Hornsley's office. They started out all nice and polite, at least from what we could hear. But before long, Mr. Hilliard was screamin' like a madman and threatening all sorts of things.''

''What exactly did he threaten?'' Barnes asked. He hoped that Nivens was getting this same information out of Frampton, but he doubted it.

''He was goin' to call his solicitors and sue, then he was goin' to tell everyone what a blackguard Mr. Hornsley was, finally,'' the clerk's voice dropped, ''as he was leaving, he yelled that Mr. Hornsley had better watch his back.''

Mrs. Jeffries took a seat at the table and looked around the crowded tea room. There was no one she recognized and more importantly, no one who would know who she was. She smiled at the waiter and ordered tea for two. A moment later, the door opened and in stepped Dr. Bosworth, an attractive young man of about thirty, with dark red hair and a fair complexion.

He spotted her quickly and threaded his way to her table. "Good day, Mrs. Jeffries," he said, giving her a smile.

"Good day, Dr. Bosworth." She gestured at a chair. "Won't you sit down? I've taken the liberty of ordering tea."

"Thank you," he sat down. "I haven't much time but as your note said it was a matter of some urgency, I decided to see you."

"I think you know why I asked you to come," she said. She'd decided not to beat about the bush. Dr. Bosworth had helped them with several other cases and his opinions had proved invaluable.

"Indeed I do," he replied. He broke off as the waiter brought them tea and cakes. Mrs. Jeffries poured. "You want to ask me what I know about the Hornsley murder."

"Right. I was hoping you might have done the post-mortem." She picked up her own cup and took a sip.

"No such luck," Dr. Bosworth sighed. "Potter did that one."

"Oh dear," Mrs. Jeffries was disappointed. Dr. Potter was a plodding, unimaginative, and rather stupid man who could barely distinguish a bullet hole from a stab wound. "How unfortunate."

"How tactful you are." Bosworth laughed. "Don't worry, Mrs. Jeffries. As soon as I heard the circumstances of the killing, I nipped over to the morgue and had a look-see for myself."

She brightened immediately. "And what did you conclude?"

"Actually," Bosworth said slowly, "I concluded the

same thing that Potter had. The victim was struck on the back of the head and then strangled with a house tie.''

"A house tie?"

"Yes." Bosworth reached for a fairy cake. "Knowing how very interested you are in getting all the details straight, when I got a good look at the actual murder weapon, I realized it was a school tie. Then I got curious so I made a few discreet inquiries on my own. Voilà, it wasn't just a school tie, but a house tie.''

"Bravo, sir,'' Mrs. Jeffries beamed approvingly. "We'll make a detective out of you yet.''

He laughed again. "I daresay, it was probably because of my acquaintance with you that got me started in this whole business. I am, after all, just a doctor. But I must admit, your little adventures and my small part in them does seem to have had some influence on me. Anyway, as I was saying, I made some inquiries when I saw the murder weapon. Curious object for a killer to use.''

"What did you find out?'' she asked eagerly.

"The tie is from a public school near Oxford,'' he explained. "One of those especially hideous places where we send our male children to be systematically tortured between the ages of seven and eighteen.''

Surprised at the vehemence in his voice, she stared at him. "Why, Dr. Bosworth, am I to take that to mean that you don't approve of our education system?''

"I think it's barbaric,'' he said with feeling. "Stupid, ridiculous, and utterly absurd. Having been a victim of a particularly loathsome school myself, I know what I'm talking about.'' Shaking his head in disgust, he leaned back in his chair. "If I ever have children, I'll never send them away to school. I'll keep them at home and let them go to a good day school, like the Americans do. You know I spent quite a bit of time in America?''

She did know. It was because of his time in San Francisco and the proliferation of violent deaths in that city that had given them a valuable clue in the first case he'd helped them on. ''Yes, I remember you mentioned that.''

''I know everyone likes to think the Americans are uneducated barbarians, but it's not true. The Americans don't send their children off to school to be tortured the way we do in this country. Not that they're perfect, of course, but they aren't quite the country bumpkins we like to think they are. And I didn't notice that their young men were any stupider for having been deprived of the fagging system. As far as I could tell, they were perfectly able to read and write and think.''

''I'm quite sure you're right.''

''But that's beside the point.'' He waved a hand dismissively. ''As I was saying, the tie is from a public school. Packards.''

''Do you know what house?'' she asked hopefully.

''It took a bit of doing, but I managed,'' he grinned. ''It's from Langley House.''

''Goodness, Doctor, you are resourceful.''

''Thank you.'' He reached for a cake. ''I do try.''

''Was there anything else you learned about the victim that might be important?''

Bosworth chewed thoughtfully. ''There are virtually no signs of a struggle. Once the poor fellow was coshed, the killer had a clear field. Hornsley didn't struggle with his murderer. There are no bruises on the hands, and the ligature around the neck is absolutely straight.''

''I suppose then that the killer probably thought he'd killed Hornsley with the blow to his head and when he realized he hadn't, he must have used the tie at that point,'' she mused. Her expression was thoughtful. ''Apparently our killer is a very careful man. He brought along a second weapon in case the first didn't work.''

''I suspect the murderer didn't plan on the blow doing anything except what it actually did,'' Bosworth replied. ''The blow wasn't hard enough to kill, only to stun.''

''Then why not just strangle the victim in the first place?'' Mrs. Jeffries queried.

''Because Hornsley was a good-sized man,'' Bosworth explained. ''Unless the murderer were very lucky, very tall, or very strong, he had to stun him with something. Even with a tie choking your windpipe, a man could still defend himself. Besides,'' he waved a hand in the air. ''Head wounds bleed something awful. That's fairly common knowledge. If he'd kept bashing the man's head in, the killer would have been covered with blood.''

''Yes,'' she agreed. ''Apparently our killer thought it out most carefully.''

''And you must admit, an old tie is a perfectly marvelous way to kill someone,'' Bosworth continued. ''It's one of those things that no one even misses from a household. Why, I've no idea where my old school ties have gone. Into the rubbish bin, I hope.''

She smiled. ''I'm sorry. It sounds as though your school days were terrible.''

''They were hideous,'' he agreed. ''Do you know, I still

loathe one of the boys who used to bully me. I ran into the chap a while back, he'd grown into a rabbity sort of fellow. Came up and tried to shake my hand. I could barely bring myself to be polite to the man.''

"Sometimes the things of childhood are the most difficult to let go of," she suggested gently. "I suppose it's because as children we have so little power or control over our lives."

"You're helpless when you're a child," Bosworth said slowly, his expression troubled. "I was quite ashamed of my reaction to Pomfret. I'm sure he'd no idea why I was so rude. But I couldn't help myself." He suddenly straightened and smiled ruefully. "But I survived. It's a wretched system, though. Can't think why we still have it."

"I rather agree with you," Mrs. Jeffries said. "Do you have any idea what the killer used to strike the blow?"

Bosworth dropped his gaze and stared at the half-eaten cake on his plate. "I'm not really sure," he mumbled. "I mean, it's almost impossible to tell . . ."

She knew he was hiding something. Dr. Bosworth was very intelligent, very observant, and not in the least afraid of educated guesses.

"But surely you've some idea," she pressed. "The wound must have been a certain size, a certain shape, a . . ."

He sighed. "Mrs. Jeffries, you know that many physicians don't believe you can tell much by examining wounds."

"I also know that you're not one of them," she argued. "You identified the kind of weapon that was used to kill that American last year merely by examining the bullet wound.''

"Yes, but that was just a guess and my statement wouldn't have stood up in a court of law.''

"Nevertheless, you were right," she said firmly. "So please, tell me what you *think* could have been used.''

He hesitated for a moment, then came to a decision. Squaring his shoulders he looked her straight in the eye. "The blow didn't actually crack the victim's skull, but it was hard enough to leave a strong indention.''

"And that means you know the general shape of the object that made the wound," she said. "Correct?''

"Yes, that's correct. But remember, there are a variety of objects of the same shape and size and weight that could cause the kind of indention that I observed.''

Mrs. Jeffries thought he was hedging. "I understand that. As you said, Doctor, you're not in the witness box. All I want is an educated guess.''

"The wound was rounded and approximately two and a half inches in diameter.''

She waited.

He took a deep breath. "It could well have been done by a police truncheon. As a matter of fact, I borrowed one from one of the constables and placed it against the victim's skull. It was a perfect fit.''

CHAPTER 4

Barnes couldn't believe they were back at Peter Hornsley's home. Why on earth hadn't Nivens had the sense to find out where Nyles Hornsley lived before rushing them both all over London and wasting time. He shot his superior an irritable glance.

Nivens was staring at a pair of silver candlesticks on the top of the marble mantle. "They're worth a bob or two," Nivens muttered. He glanced around the room, his gaze stopping at the windows. "And those locks wouldn't keep a professional out for more than ten seconds. The Hornsleys are lucky they haven't been robbed. There's plenty in here that's worth taking."

Barnes remembered that Nivens was considered somewhat of an expert on robbery. Too bad the man didn't know the first thing about homicide.

"Inspector Nivens?"

Both policemen turned toward the door. A young man of medium height and with a slight build stepped into the room. He wore a black suit and white shirt. His sandy-colored hair was parted on the side and his pale face was clean shaven. He stared at them out of wary hazel eyes.

"I'm Nyles Hornsley," he said. "I take it you're here to talk to me about my brother's murder."

"Yes, sir," Nivens replied, "we are."

"I'm surprised you didn't speak to me earlier," Hornsley said. He walked over to the settee, gestured for the policemen to sit down in the chairs opposite, and then sat down. "I was upstairs waiting for you when you were questioning Glynis."

Nivens cast Barnes a quick look and cleared his throat. "We had another matter to attend to," he explained. "A rather urgent matter as it turned out."

What a ruddy liar, Barnes thought contemptuously. Nivens would have done better to explain nothing. It was bad form to start off an interview with a suspect by explaining your actions.

Hornsley continued to stare. "Have you made any progress on catching Peter's killer?"

"We're working on it, sir." Nivens gave him a weak smile. "Now, if you don't mind, sir, I'd like to ask you a few questions."

"That's why I'm here."

"Do you know if your brother had any enemies?"

Barnes gritted his teeth. They already knew that Peter Hornsley had lots of enemies. Nivens was going 'round in blooming circles. Why didn't he ask him something useful?

"My brother was a successful businessman," Hornsley

said slowly. "There were a number of his competitors who disliked him."

"Had he ever been threatened?" Nivens asked.

Barnes shifted impatiently, earning him a disapproving frown from his superior.

"Not that I'm aware of," Hornsley replied. "But Peter rarely confided in me. We weren't close. Peter is, was, a lot older than I am. He was almost grown when I was born."

Barnes couldn't stand it anymore. "What about Damon Hilliard? Hadn't he threatened your brother?" He ignored the frown Nivens cast his way.

Hornsley looked amused. "Oh, I'd hardly call that a threat. Hilliard was just upset. Peter had undercut the poor fellow so badly he couldn't possibly compete. But Peter and his partners were always doing that sort of thing."

"What sort of thing?" Barnes pressed. The side of his face burned where Nivens was glaring at him, but the constable didn't much care. Nivens wasn't the only copper at the Yard who had a friend or two in high places. If they were going to catch this killer, someone had to start asking decent questions.

"Bribery. Peter's favorite trick was to find a clerk in a competing firm's office, give him a few bob to find out what the firm was quoting, and then undercut it by at least ten percent."

"But how could your brother stay in business if he was quoting such low insurance rates?" Barnes asked. He wasn't just curious, he really wanted to know. Supposedly the firm made pots of money, but he didn't see how that could be possible if they were always quoting below-cost rates.

"Volume," Nyles Hornsley smiled slyly. "They did an enormous amount of business. They were going to expand, you know." Hornsley waved a hand as though the matter were of no importance. "But, as I said, Peter and his partners did that all the time. They've been doing it for years. I hardly think his competitors would wait till now to kill him. It would have been much more useful if they'd murdered him a year ago."

"And why is that, sir?" Barnes asked.

"Excuse me, Constable," Nivens snapped. "But I'm asking the questions here."

"Sorry, sir," Barnes said, but he continued to stare at Hornsley, silently trying to get him to answer. He was disappointed.

Nivens cleared his throat in that irritating way he had. "Now, Mr. Hornsley, did your brother do anything out of the ordinary on the day he was killed?"

"Not that I'm aware of."

"Did he give any indication of being frightened?"

Hornsley laughed. "No. My brother had far too high an opinion of himself to act like the rest of us mere mortals. Even if he'd had a dozen notes threatening him, he wouldn't have given any outward sign. He was simply too arrogant."

Ask Nyles Hornsley where he was the night of the murder, Barnes silently screamed. He had an awful feeling that Nivens was going to stop asking questions. Ask him if he knows anything about the note. Ask him about Madeline Wynn. Ask him what VENI might mean.

"Well." Nivens rose to his feet. "I do thank you for your help, Mr. Hornsley. If we've any news, we'll be in touch."

Barnes silently groaned. Silly git. At this rate, they were never going to catch the killer. The thought made him furious. The constable realized that the two and a half years he'd spent working with Witherspoon had changed him. His sense of justice was outraged. A murderer was going to go free because of an incompetent police inspector with more friends in high places than sense.

Barnes simply couldn't stand it. "Excuse me, Mr. Hornsley, but would you mind telling us where you were last night?"

"I don't mind in the least," he smiled. "I was at the Alexandra Hotel. My fiancée and I were having dinner with some friends."

"And what time did you arrive at the Alexandra?" Barnes prodded.

"Let me see," Hornsley replied thoughtfully. "I went round to Madeline's about half-past six. We had a glass of sherry with her aunt and then took a hansom to the Alexandra. I'd say we arrived there at seven-fifteen or seven-thirty."

"And the names of the friends you dined with?" Barnes could sense that Nivens was furious, but he didn't care.

"Mr. and Mrs. Arthur Stanley." Hornsley smiled widely. "We were with them until ten o'clock. You can verify it, if you like. The Stanleys live at number twelve Lanham Street. That's in Mayfair."

"Thank you, sir," Barnes said formally. "We will be in touch with them." He would have loved to ask Hornsley

more questions, but he was afraid that Nivens would interrupt. Well, there was more than one way to skin a cat. He'd
find out what he needed to know without Nigel Nivens
around to muck things up!

As soon as they were outside, Nivens turned to Barnes.
"In the future," he said coldly, "I'll thank you not to interfere."

"Sorry, sir." Barnes tried to look contrite. "But I was
only doing what I always do."

Nivens's eyes narrowed suspiciously. "What do you
mean?"

"I mean, sir, that when I'm with Inspector Witherspoon,
I'm expected to toss in a few questions. For effect, sir.
That's what Inspector Witherspoon says. Claims it gets
people talking more, tellin' a bit more than they really
wanted to, if you know what I mean. Interestin' method,
isn't it?" Barnes smiled blandly.

Nivens pursed his thin lips as though he were seriously
thinking about the constable's words. Finally, he said,
"That's all well and good, Constable. But I'm not Inspector
Witherspoon . . ."

That's a fact, Barnes thought.

". . . and my methods are very, very different." Nivens
started down the stone stairs toward the street. "And hence-
forth, I'll expect you to keep your mouth shut and take
notes. Is that clear?"

"Very, sir."

Mrs. Jeffries was deep in thought as she walked down
Adam Street. Dr. Bosworth's information was most helpful.
Obviously, the killer had thought everything out in ad-

vance. But she already knew that. Equally obvious was the fact that he'd brought two weapons along. One to stun and one to kill. But why a police truncheon? The killer was masquerading as Inspector Witherspoon, a detective. But Witherspoon didn't even carry one. She wondered where the inspector's truncheon was? Hopefully, it was somewhere in his room at Upper Edmonton Gardens.

Mrs. Jeffries was so lost in thought she didn't notice the two men coming down the stairs just a few feet in front of her. When the sound of a familiar voice finally penetrated her musing, she came to an abrupt halt.

"Good day, Inspector Nivens, Constable Barnes." She forced herself to smile calmly. Oh dear, what on earth was she going to say to them? She glanced quickly up and down the elegant row of houses desperately hoping to see a fishmonger's or a greengrocer's on one of the corners. But there was nothing save more homes. Drat.

"Mrs. Jeffries," Nivens eyed her suspiciously. "What are you doing here?"

Barnes gazed at her impassively, but she could see the curiosity in his eyes.

"Actually," she smiled again, "I was looking for you."

Nivens blinked in surprise. "Really. Why?"

She hesitated. "It's rather presumptuous of me," she began, thinking fast, "but the household is very worried."

"Worried about what?" Nivens asked, his fish-eyed gaze never leaving her face.

"About the inspector," she replied. "We're concerned because, well, we were wondering if . . . oh dear, this is most improper, but you see, we're so very worried."

Nivens waved his hand impatiently. "Yes, you've already said that. Now what is it, Mrs. Jeffries? I've not got all day. We've a murderer to catch.''

Barnes grinned.

Mrs. Jeffries took a deep breath. "We're wondering if Scotland Yard really thinks Inspector Witherspoon has anything to do with this awful murder.''

Nivens's mouth dropped open.

Mrs. Jeffries wondered if it was because of her audacity or because he was just inherently too arrogant and stupid to comprehend that servants would actually be devoted enough to an employer to care.

"Well, really, I don't think that is any of your household's concern," Nivens sputtered.

"But it is our concern," she countered, looking him straight in the eye. This was no time to be timid. Nivens was a bit of a bully, and if he sensed you were the least bit frightened or intimidated, he'd be on you like a starving rat. "We're all very devoted to the inspector. Furthermore, we know good and well he's nothing to do with this murder. If you don't feel like addressing our concerns, sir, that's quite all right. I'm sure Chief Inspector Curling wouldn't mind speaking with me. He's such a very nice man.''

They stared at one another for a good minute. Nivens was weighing the consequences of her running and having a chat with his superior and she was holding her breath, hoping her bluff would work.

Nivens dropped his gaze first. "Of course Witherspoon isn't considered a serious suspect. I'm amazed you'd actually be concerned about such a thing.''

Graciously, she smiled. "As I said, we're very devoted to the inspector."

"Then perhaps you'd best convince him to tell us the truth," Nivens said. He smiled coldly when he saw her start with surprise.

"The truth? About what?"

"About where he was and what he was doing the evening of March ninth. The night of the murder."

As it was only a few days ago, Mrs. Jeffries rather thought that Nivens was being pedantic. "He was taking a walk," she said quickly. "He's already told you that."

"He might well have been walking." Nivens shrugged. "But he wasn't walking where he said he was. He was nowhere near Holland Park between half-past six and eight o'clock that night."

"How can you possibly be sure of that?"

"But I am sure," Nivens said flatly. "You see, we've had a rash of purse snatchings in that area. So we had constables on all the pathways leading into and out of the park. Inspector Witherspoon is well known." His voice dripped sarcasm. "After all, he is considered Scotland Yard's most successful homicide detective. God knows he gets his name in the newspapers often enough. Both his name and his face are familiar to most of the lads."

She swallowed uneasily. "Are you saying that none of those constables saw him that night?"

"That's right," Nivens replied casually. "Not one of them. And believe me, if he'd been there, someone would have seen him. Furthermore, they'd have remembered him. As I said, he's quite famous."

"But Inspector Witherspoon had no reason to murder Peter Hornsley," she pointed out.

"True." Nivens picked a piece of lint off his sleeve. "But motive is one of the last things we look for in a case of this sort."

Mrs. Jeffries wasn't sure, but she thought she heard Barnes snort. Nivens must have thought so too. He gave the constable a sharp look.

"I'm sure there's been some kind of mistake about this," Mrs. Jeffries murmured. She looked at the constable. He nodded his head slightly in agreement. "If Inspector Witherspoon said he was walking in Holland Park that night, then I'm sure that's precisely where he was."

"Hmm. Yes, well, I do hope there's some reasonable explanation," Nivens replied.

"Perhaps he got confused as to where he actually did walk," Mrs. Jeffries suggested. "After all, it was quite dark and foggy that night. The inspector goes out walking quite often. He could easily have gotten confused. He might well have been walking in Holland Park the night before the murder and somewhere else the night of the murder."

"Really, Mrs. Jeffries"—Nivens's lip curled in a sneer—"Inspector Witherspoon isn't a fool. He knows perfectly well how important an alibi is in a murder investigation. It's not likely he'd get mixed up about something like that. We are talking about an incident from three days back, not three weeks."

"I know there's some explanation for it," she insisted. No matter what she said, she was sure Nivens wasn't going to believe her.

"Let's hope so. But please, do tell the rest of the household that your dear Inspector Witherspoon isn't seriously a suspect.'' He gave her another cold smile. ''Not yet, anyway.''

Mrs. Goodge was in the kitchen when Mrs. Jeffries returned. The cook gave her a short greeting and then went back to cutting up the meat for her stew.

Mrs. Jeffries wasn't in the chattiest of moods herself. When she'd returned home, she'd found the inspector sitting in the drawing room, with an open book on his lap. She'd asked him why he wasn't out investigating the robbery; he'd told her that there was no need. Last night, one of the uniformed lads had interrupted a break-in at a home in Carlton Square. The robbers had confessed to the other burglaries as well. So now the inspector was taking a few days' rest. In other words, he was going to be under their feet.

''Did the inspector tell you his robbery was solved?'' Mrs. Jeffries said to the cook.

''He told me.'' Mrs. Goodge didn't look up from her task. ''Do you want a cup of tea now, or will you wait till the others get here?''

''I'll wait.'' She sighed silently. Unfortunately, she'd also asked the inspector about his walk on the night of the murder. Naturally, she'd been most discreet about her inquiry. He insisted he'd been walking in Holland Park, but he hadn't been able to look her in the eyes while saying so.

She knew, then, that he was lying.

''I believe I will have that cup of tea, after all,'' Mrs. Jeffries murmured. Why wouldn't he tell her where he'd been? It wasn't like Inspector Witherspoon to deceive. It simply wasn't in the man's character, yet he was lying through his teeth on this matter.

"Suit yourself."

"Can I make you one?" she asked Mrs. Goodge.

The cook shook her head. Mrs. Jeffries put the kettle on and then pulled her favorite cup out of the cupboard.

Oh dear, this case was most worrying, she thought. Most worrying indeed. She forced her imagination to stay in check. There was absolutely no reason why Gerald Witherspoon, highly respected police detective with Scotland Yard, would take it into his head to murder a perfectly innocent stranger.

But was Peter Hornsley a stranger? The uneasy idea crept into her mind before she could stop it. How much did she really know about her employer? How much did any of them really know about each other?

The kettle whistled, interrupting her train of thought. "Are you sure you wouldn't like a cup?" she said, glancing over at the cook. She noticed the cook's shoulders were slumped and her face was set in a worried frown.

"Is there anything the matter, Mrs. Goodge?" she asked. "You seem awfully quiet this afternoon."

"Oh, I wouldn't say anything was exactly wrong," said Mrs. Goodge as she put her knife down and wiped her hands on a towel. "I believe I will have that tea," she sighed. "Maybe talking about it will help me to come to a decision."

Mrs. Jeffries poured them both a cup and they took their usual spots at the table. "Why don't you tell me what's upsetting you?"

"Nothing's really upsettin' me," the cook said slowly.

"Actually, one part of me is quite pleased. It's just now I'm in a muddle and I don't know what to do."

"Why, Mrs. Goodge, you're never in a muddle," Mrs. Jeffries said earnestly.

"This time I am." She toyed with the handle of her cup. "You see, I've had a letter from one of my old employers. He wants me to come back and work for him. It's Lord Gurney."

Mrs. Jeffries stared at her. She knew how much the cook enjoyed status. And cooking for a lord of the realm would have far more cachet than cooking for a Scotland Yard detective, even a wealthy, famous one like Inspector Witherspoon. "And what have you decided to do?"

"That's just it," Mrs. Goodge cried. "I don't know what to do. I like it here. I like helping to solve murders and having all of you round and about the kitchen. It's a far different thing working for a lord. There I'd be head cook with scullery and serving girls under me. I'd get my tea brought up to my room each mornin' and not have to do any of the peeling or chopping of the vegetables. There's a strict way of doin' things in Lord Gurney's house. I can tell you that."

"I see," Mrs. Jeffries murmured. "Well, why don't you have a good think about it before you make up your mind?"

Mrs. Goodge nodded. "Right strange, isn't it? How something from the past you think is over and done with can come creeping up on you like a thief in the night. When I left Lord Gurney's employment, I never thought I'd set foot in that house again. Yet here he is, a few years later, writing me letters asking me to come back."

"Yoo-hoo," came Luty Belle Crookshank's voice from the backdoor.

"Really, madam, that's hardly a proper way to announce our presence," Hatchet chided his employer.

"What'd you want me to do," Luty snapped, "blast a trumpet like we was the heavenly hosts?"

"Hello, Luty, Hatchet," Mrs. Jeffries said quickly as the two of them came into the kitchen. "Do sit down. We'll have some tea ready shortly."

Mrs. Goodge got up. "I'll put it on."

"Good," Luty nodded. "I'm as dry as a river gully in a California desert."

They heard the sound of thumping coming from the back stairs and a moment later, Wiggins, with Fred at his heels, hobbled to the table. "I've 'ad a borin' day," he announced. "My eyes is crossed from readin' and polishin' and me ears are ringin' from listening to Essie go on about the rights of the workers."

Luty cackled. "That Essie's a right talker, isn't she?"

Hatchet harrumphed softly. "Should we wait for the others?" he asked.

Mrs. Jeffries shook her head. "No, we'd best get on with it. The inspector is upstairs, reading. He's rather upset. He told me not to worry about getting his dinner; he said he wasn't hungry. Poor man, this case is weighing heavily on his mind. So let's get started while we've got the chance. We can fill Betsy and Smythe in after our own meal this evening."

Darkness had come, even though it was only a little past five. Mrs. Goodge, uncharacteristically silent, poured tea and handed round slices of cake.

"Who would like to go first?" Mrs. Jeffries queried.

"Why don't we start?" Luty said. "I think Hatchet's got somethin' to say."

"That I do, madam." The butler cleared his throat. "As you know, I've a number of sources I can draw upon when the circumstances call for it."

"Yes, yes, we all know about that," Luty said impatiently. "You've told us often enough. Just go ahead and tell us what you've found out."

"Don't rush me, madam," Hatchet replied irritably. "I want to make sure I tell this calmly and clearly. A muddled set of facts is worse than no facts at all. Anyway, as I was saying, I prevailed upon one of my sources to inquire as to the whereabouts of the various members of Peter Hornsley's household at the time of the murder."

"You mean you bribed a butler or a housemaid to spill the beans," Luty said.

Outraged, Hatchet glared at her. "I most certainly did not."

"Don't be such a stuffed shirt," Luty shot back. "There ain't nothin' wrong with crossin' someone's palm with silver if they can tell ya what ya need to know. Anyways, get on with it. We haven't got all day."

Mrs. Jeffries would have intervened to smooth things out, but these two enjoyed sparring with one another even more than they enjoyed investigating murders.

"As I was saying," Hatchet continued. "My sources told me something very interesting. At the time of the murder, Mrs. Hornsley was not at home. Nor was she having tea with Mrs. Frampton, which was where she'd told her husband she was going late that afternoon. As a matter of fact, she didn't get home till past eight that night. So you see, she doesn't have an alibi."

"Does she have a motive?" Mrs. Jeffries asked.

Luty cackled. "Course she had a motive, I found that out. I had a long chat with my friend Myrtle while Hatchet was out today. Accordin' to Myrtle, Glynis Hornsley was this close"—she held up her thumb and finger, leaving a tiny space between them—"to getting a divorce from Peter Hornsley. She hated his guts."

"A divorce!" Mrs. Goodge said incredulously. "But that's . . . that's . . . unheard of. Only actresses and opera singers get divorced."

"That's not true," Wiggins put in. "There was over seven thousand divorces done last year, and they couldn't have all been opera singers."

They all turned and stared at the footman.

"How on earth do you know that?" Mrs. Jeffries asked curiously.

Wiggins shrugged. "I read about it somewheres. But I know it's true."

Mrs. Jeffries had no doubt about that. Wiggins might be a bit of a daydreamer, but he was certainly no liar. "How very interesting," she smiled at him. "And how very clever of you to remember it."

"I don't believe it," Mrs. Goodge said.

"But it's true," Wiggins exclaimed. "Just because I can't remember where I read it don't mean I'm makin' it up."

"I don't mean that." The cook waved her hand. "I mean I can't believe a respectable woman like Glynis Hornsley would even think about getting a divorce. Why, she'd be ruined. Absolutely ruined. No decent people would have anything to do with her.''

''But that's what Myrtle claims,'' Luty argued. ''And believe me, Myrtle don't get her gossip wrong.''

''Did she say why Mrs. Hornsley was considering divorce?'' Mrs. Jeffries asked.

Luty shrugged. ''All she said was that the marriage hadn't been happy in years. Glynis didn't much like her husband. Maybe she wanted to get shut of the fellow so she could have a bit of peace and quiet. Myrtle says he was a right domineerin' sort, always onto his wife about something. Then there was the woman he kept, but accordin' to Myrtle, Mrs. Hornsley didn't much care about that.'' She laughed. ''Seems the marriage really started to go sour when Hornsley's mistress left him and he started comin' home more often.''

''That lets her out as a suspect, then,'' Wiggins said firmly. ''Why would she bother to kill 'im if she was fixin' to get herself divorced?''

''Not necessarily,'' Hatchet shook his head. ''As Mrs. Goodge pointed out, if she divorced him, she'd be risking social ruin.''

''But we know it was a man that killed Hornsley,'' Luty said.

''Not necessarily,'' Mrs. Jeffries said. ''We know that a man claiming to be Inspector Witherspoon was one of the last people to be seen with Hornsley. That doesn't mean he killed him.''

''But it had to be him,'' Mrs. Goodge pointed out. ''There was a night watchman on duty. No one else came into the building.''

Mrs. Jeffries frowned. "Yes, I suppose that's true. But Glynis Hornsley could have easily have hired someone to murder her husband. So I don't think we ought yet to write her off as a suspect. Did you learn anything else?"

"No," Luty admitted. "That's all I got."

"Me too," Hatchet said. "But we'll keep working."

Mrs. Jeffries told them about her meeting with Dr. Bosworth, and then went on to explain the disastrous run-in with Inspector Nivens. She then took a deep breath and told them about Inspector Witherspoon's insistence that he was walking in Holland Park the night of the murder.

When she was through she glanced around the table. Luty was fingering the mink muff on her lap, Hatchet's eyebrows were drawn together in a worried frown, Mrs. Goodge was chewing on her lower lip, and Wiggins was studying the top of the table as if he could read the secrets of the ancients in its old wood.

"Well, say something," she cried. "Surely you've some idea why Inspector Witherspoon missed being seen by the constables in the park."

Wiggins looked up, his cheeks flushed a fiery red. "I don't see how he rightly could," he said softly. "I mean, if the police were there, and we've no reason to think Nivens would lie about that, then they shoulda seen 'im."

"I think it's apparent that Inspector Witherspoon wasn't walking in Holland Park that night," Hatchet said carefully. "Perhaps he was confused. I mean, perhaps he'd been in the park the night before and got his evenings mixed up."

"I already asked him about that," Mrs. Jeffries sighed. She didn't like the tone of this conversation, but she couldn't run away from the truth because it was uncomfortable. "He insists he was there."

"Do you think Inspector Witherspoon could kill someone?" Luty asked bluntly.

"Of course not," Mrs. Jeffries replied. "Besides, even if he could, why murder a complete stranger?"

"If he was a stranger," Wiggins muttered.

"What do you mean by that?" Mrs. Jeffries demanded.

"I mean . . ." Wiggins hesitated. "How much do we know about the inspector? Before a couple of years ago, we'd never laid eyes on each other. For all we know, Peter Hornsley weren't no stranger to our inspector."

"Bloomin' fog," Betsy glared at the pearly mist as she hurried down the road. "I'll never find a hansom in this soup," she muttered. Not that she could normally afford hansoms, but it was already dark and she was in a rush to get home. She had so much to tell everyone. Mind you, she thought as she quickened her pace, her heels clicking smartly against the wet stone pavement, it was clever of me to remember to take those coins out of my drawer. At least if I can find a hansom, I can afford the fare. She frowned and her footsteps slowed as she remembered how surprised she'd been when she'd opened the top drawer of her bureau to grab her money. There was more money in the drawer than there should have been.

Betsy shook her head. She was getting as forgetful as Mrs. Goodge. She must have put more in there than she'd thought. She always kept a few shillings and pence out of her quarterly pay, and this time she'd obviously kept more than she normally did. That had to be the answer. It wasn't likely there was anyone else dropping money in the drawer. But it is puzzlin', she thought. And it's not the first time things like that have happened around the house. Wiggins findin' some brand-new expensive writin' paper in his drawer, Mrs. Goodge's rheumatism bottle always gettin' replaced before she finished it, Mrs. Jeffries finding the new Whitman poems in her bookcase. Why, the only one who hadn't had a nice surprise was Smythe. From behind her, someone grabbed her elbow and spun her around.

Betsy screamed. Her eyes widened as she found herself looking straight into a face she hoped she'd never see again. "You!"

"Hello, Betsy," Raymond Skegit smiled broadly, revealing a set of perfect white teeth. "It's been a long time."

"Not long enough," Betsy jerked her arm away and stepped back. Despite her bravado, she was scared. "I'd hoped never to see you again."

He was a tall, thin man in his late twenties, clean shaven and dark haired. A handsome bloke, the kind that turned women's heads and made men stare at him with envy.

"You don't mean that, girl," he said, still smiling, but the look in his eyes sent a chill up Betsy's spine. "You're lucky I'm not one to take offense. Otherwise, my feelin's would get hurt. You don't want to hurt my feelin's, Betsy. Not again."

She stepped back further, hating herself for retreating but unwilling to stay close enough for him to get his hands on her—again. She glanced up the road. Not a copper in sight. Blast. Where were they when you needed one? Well, if she had to, she'd scream her head off.

"I couldn't care less about your bleedin' feelin's," she

retorted, hating the way her voice trembled and the way her speech had slipped into pure cockney. "Now, if you'll get out of my way, I'll be off," she forced herself to speak properly. "I'm in a hurry."

Raymond laughed. "That's no way to treat an old friend." He came closer, his mouth curling in an ugly way. "And we are old friends, Betsy. Even if you'd like to pretend you've never laid eyes on me before."

"We was never friends," she snapped. She'd have to make a run for it. "The likes of you don't have 'friends,' Raymond. No decent person would have anything to do with someone like you."

"Yeah, but you did, didn't ya? You come to me that night and asked me to take ya on." He gave up all pretense at smiling, his expression now hard and menacing. "Then, before we could do any business together, ya took off. I didn't like that, Betsy. I didn't like it at all. It weren't right." He grabbed her arm. "And I think you'd best come with me. You've got to make amends."

"Let go of me," Betsy tried to jerk her arm free, but his grip was too tight. He started dragging her down the street. In the fog ahead, she could make out a waiting carriage. "Let go of me, ya bastard," she yelled. "Or I'll scream me 'ead off."

"You there," Smythe's bellow came from directly behind them. "Take yer bloody 'ands off 'er."

Raymond stopped. Betsy yanked her arm free and turned in the direction of the coachman's voice. She ran for him like the devil himself was on her heels.

Smythe charged out of the fog. His big hands came out and he grabbed Betsy as she came hurtling toward him. He pushed her behind him. "Stay there," he ordered. "I'll take care of this bastard."

Raymond, who'd for a brief instant considered trying to reclaim his prize, took one look at the huge, brutal-looking man who'd emerged from the fog and changed his mind. Before the enraged man could reach him, he turned and ran for the carriage.

Smythe started after him, but Betsy grabbed his arm. "Let him go," she cried.

"But he's gettin' away," Smythe yelled, torn between wanting to get his hands on that bastard and wanting to stay to make sure she was all right.

"I don't care. Just let him go," she pleaded.

By this time, Skegit's carriage had taken off at a fast clip. Smythe put his hands on his hips and turned to Betsy. "Who the blazes was that?" he demanded. "And why was he trying to drag you off?"

CHAPTER 5

George Frampton elbowed his way through the crowded saloon bar of the Black Horse Pub. Usually he would have gone into one of the private sections of the pub, but tonight he wanted to be around people. He was nervous.

Reaching the counter, he slapped his money on the polished wood. "Whiskey," he said to the publican. "And make it quick."

Frampton let himself relax a bit as the barman got his order. God, he needed a drink. Needed it more than any other night he'd stopped in here on his way home. He drew a deep breath into his lungs, enjoying the acrid smell of cigar smoke and the scent of bitter and mild ale. The noise level was deafening. Frampton took great comfort in being in the midst of the crowded room. Not that he was seriously worried about being murdered, no, of course not.

"Thanks," he said as the publican put his drink down. He took a long swig of the good Irish whiskey, enjoying the burning sensation as it rolled down his throat and hit his belly. It wasn't that he was frightened, he told himself. But it made sense to be a bit cautious. There was a killer out there.

The police didn't seem to have any idea about who'd murdered Peter. Frampton frowned, thinking about the interview he'd had this morning with that police inspector. The man didn't seem to be too bright. He didn't ask very many questions. Frampton wasn't sure that they would ever find the murderer.

Peter had a lot of enemies. Far more than he'd let on to the police this morning, that was for sure. Frampton sighed, wishing he could feel some real grief for his partner's death. But the truth was, he didn't feel much of anything. He should have. He really should have felt something. He and Peter had gone to school together, known each other for years. But it wasn't as if Peter had been a nice person, he thought defensively. Or even a decent one. He'd always been a mean, arrogant man. Bullying those who were weaker and bluffing those that got in his way. But still, Frampton wished he could feel something other than this emptiness.

The door of the pub opened, letting in a blast of cold, damp air. Frampton felt the wind against the back of his neck, but he didn't turn to see who had just walked in. He finished his drink.

Slapping the glass on the counter, he'd opened his mouth to shout at the barman for another one when a man appeared at his elbow. The fellow was wearing a large dark overcoat, bowler hat, and spectacles. He had a mustache.

"Mr. Frampton?" he queried politely.

"Yes," he replied cautiously. "Who are you?"

"Inspector Gerald Witherspoon, Scotland Yard." The man said firmly. He smiled thinly as Frampton started in surprise. "Don't be alarmed, sir. I assure you, I'm not a murderer, despite having had someone use my name in such a vile manner."

Frampton relaxed slightly. "Well, all right, I suppose . . ."

"Don't worry, Mr. Frampton," Inspector Witherspoon said heartily. "Scotland Yard would hardly let me walk about free if they really suspected I had anything to do with your partner's death."

"What about that other fellow I talked to this morning? Chap named Nivens," Frampton asked. "Why isn't he here?"

"Inspector Nivens is no longer on this case," Witherspoon shrugged. "It happens that way sometimes. Chief Inspector Curling didn't feel enough progress was being made so he called me in." He smiled modestly. "I'm rather well known for solving difficult homicides, if I do say so myself."

"Yes, well, I hope so," Frampton said. "That other fellow didn't even ask me many questions."

"That's why I'm here. That, of course, and some other matters that are urgent."

Frampton straightened up. "Urgent? What's this about then?"

Witherspoon glanced around the crowded room. "Are you ready to leave, sir? There is something I need to speak to you about and I'd rather not do so in here."

"I've finished." Frampton decided he'd have another

drink at home. "I only live across the park. If you like, we can talk there."

"That would be excellent, sir." Witherspoon smiled gratefully.

Nodding to the barman, who'd been listening with avid interest to their conversation, Frampton and Witherspoon left the pub.

Outside, the fog had gotten heavier. They crossed Knightsbridge, dodging hansoms and drays. Witherspoon took the lead, walking briskly toward the entrance to Hyde Park that lay just across the next road. Frampton slowed his steps. He looked to his left and saw a vicar going up the walkway into Holy Trinity Church. "Uh, excuse me, Inspector?"

Witherspoon turned. "Yes?"

"Perhaps we ought to go round the other way. I'm not certain it's safe for us to go into the park."

"That won't be necessary, sir," Witherspoon said cheerfully. "You're quite safe. It's important that you don't vary your routine. You take this shortcut through the park every evening, don't you?"

"Yes." Frampton looked at him warily. "But how do you know that?"

"We know a lot more than you think, sir. Do please come on, you'll be safe with me. Furthermore, there are a number of other policemen in the area."

Frampton looked around him. Except for the passing carriages and cabs, there wasn't anyone about. "I don't see anyone."

The policeman smiled. "That's the whole point, sir. We've been following you since you left your office, sir," he explained. "There's half a dozen policemen watching us right now. You're not supposed to see them."

"Why have you been following me?" Frampton asked. His voice was slightly irritated, as though he'd only just thought of what else being watched by the police could mean.

"To insure your safety, sir," the policeman said as he started into Hyde Park. He walked swiftly, and his silhouette was soon disappearing through the thick yellow fog.

Frampton hurried after him. "My safety? But why?"

Witherspoon slowed his steps so that his companion could catch up with him. He glanced back the way they'd just come. The fog had closed up behind them, making it impossible to see the busy road or the park entrance.

"Have you gone deaf?" Frampton sputtered. "Answer my question. Why is Scotland Yard concerned about my safety?"

"I can hear you perfectly, sir," Witherspoon smiled coldly. "We've had word that the killer is going after you next."

Frampton's heart leapt into his throat. He looked wildly about him, hoping he'd see a whole platoon of police constables. He saw nothing but the vague shapes of trees and shrubs. "My God, and you've let me walk into this deserted park? Good God, man, the killer could be anywhere."

Frampton turned to go back the way they'd just come. He hadn't taken two steps when he felt a blinding pain in his head. He dropped to his knees, but before he could do more than moan, he was grabbed under the arms, pulled off the path and dragged behind a mound of shrubbery. He couldn't speak, he couldn't cry out in alarm. All he could do was gasp for air like some great stranded fish.

Then he felt something round his neck. A few moments later, he couldn't even gasp. George Frampton was dead.

The killer pushed Frampton's body onto the ground and rolled him onto his back. He stood up and looked around. There was no one about in the park. Quickly, he reached into his pocket for an envelope and a piece of paper, then he knelt by his victim. He slipped the envelope into the dead man's inside coat pocket. He stared at the paper for a moment, unable to see what was written there because of the darkness; he smiled, anyway. He knew what it said. Carefully, he pinned the note to the man's chest.

Standing up, he again checked the area for people, but it was still deserted. The damp, unfriendly night and the heavy fog were now his allies.

He bent down and grasped the dead man's arms. Grunting slightly, he pulled the body to the edge of the shrubbery and made sure the legs were sticking out far enough to be seen by anyone passing by.

He wanted this body to be discovered.

" 'Ave you gone deaf, Betsy?" Smythe demanded in a harsh whisper. "Who the devil was that bloke?"

Betsy leaned back against the back of the hansom. She wished Smythe wouldn't keep on at her. The sound of the horses' hooves was loud on the wet street, but not loud enough to keep her from hearing the coachman's angry questions. Questions he'd been asking since he'd hustled her into this hansom a few minutes after chasing Raymond off. "I told ya, he was nobody."

"But he knew your name," Smythe persisted. "I heard him use your name so you must 'ave known the blighter."

Betsy closed her eyes. She felt lower than a snake. Smythe had rescued her, so he deserved some answers. But how could she tell him? How could she tell anyone about Raymond Skegit? If she did, she'd have to tell about herself. And she'd die before she'd ever let Smythe know about that.

She bit her lip. "He was just someone I used to know, that's all."

Smythe glared at her. He'd been scared out of his wits when he'd come round that corner and seen the fellow draggin' Betsy off. He thanked his lucky stars he hadn't let his pride stop him from keeping an eye on the lass, despite her insistence that she could take care of herself. "Why was he tryin' to drag you off? And don't try tellin' me he weren't, I've got eyes in me 'ead. I saw he 'ad you by the arm and you was fightin' him."

Betsy sighed. She knew Smythe wouldn't let up. She decided that half a lie was better than being badgered all evening. "He's just a bloke I used to know, that's all. His name is Raymond. He'd had a bit too much to drink and he was trying to make me go to a pub with him. He wasn't going to hurt me." That was a lie. She had no doubt at all that if she'd fallen into Raymond's hands, he would have hurt her.

Smythe stared at her, his expression openly skeptical.

Betsy turned her head and stared out the narrow window. She wasn't that good an actress. God, she was shakin' like a leaf just thinking about Raymond Skegit. Smythe had eyes in his head and he was a smart man, good at putting two and two together and coming up with four. He could see that she was terrified. He could also probably see that she was lying her head off, too.

"Where do ya know 'im from?" he persisted.

"Where do you think?" she shot back. "The East End. We grew up in the same area."

"What's 'is name again?" Smythe asked. He had his own way of gettin' information. Blast a Spaniard—how could he protect the lass if she wouldn't tell him the truth?

Betsy considered lying again, but then decided against it. She'd already said the name once. He'd know if she gave him a different one now. He'd know for sure she was hidin' something. "Raymond Skegit," she mumbled.

"Where's 'e live?"

"How should I know?" Betsy snapped. "This is the first I've seen him in years."

He started to ask more questions and then clamped his mouth shut. In the dull glow of the lamplight, he could see she was deathly pale, and despite the bravado of her words, her eyes betrayed her. She was still terrified.

"Easy lass," he murmured, he reached across and patted her shoulder. "I'm only trying to 'elp. We don't want you havin' another set-to with this fellow, do we?"

Betsy gave him a weak smile. "Just let it be, Smythe. All right? I'm not likely to run into him again."

"Well, then," he lied, "if that's what you want, I'll let it alone."

He'd get word to Blimpey Groggins tomorrow. With enough money, Blimpey could find out anything. "How are ya feelin'? He didn't hurt you, did 'e? Let's see that arm, he was hangin' onto you pretty tight. Are there any bruises?'' He reached for Betsy's hand, intending to take her arm and have a good look at it.

But Betsy's fingers clamped tightly around his. Surprised, he glanced up at her. She kept her eyes closed as she leaned her head against the seat. ''My arm's fine,'' she said softly. ''He didn't hurt me. Besides, you couldn't see bruises, my sleeves are too long.''

Uncertain of what to do, Smythe started to pull away, to give her some breathin' room. But her fingers tightened around his. She held onto his hand all the way home.

Betsy and Smythe joined the others at the table. Before coming into the house, Betsy had made Smythe promise he wouldn't tell anyone what had happened.

Mrs. Jeffries watched the two of them as they took their seats. She knew something was wrong. Betsy was as white as a sheet and Smythe, despite his polite words of greeting, looked as if he wanted to take the room apart with his bare hands. ''I'm glad you made it back before the meeting broke up,'' she said. ''We were starting to get worried.''

''We're fine,'' Smythe said shortly.

''That's right,'' Betsy agreed. ''It just took a bit longer to get home than we thought. Have we missed much?''

Mrs. Jeffries told them everything that they'd talked about. ''What about you two? Who wants to go first?''

Smythe cleared his throat. ''I'll start. I found out more about why Nyles Hornsley hated his brother. Seems Nyles has a sweetheart, a woman named Madeline Wynn. Big brother doesn't approve of her. But accordin' to me source, that's not the only reason there was bad feelin's between the brothers. Peter Hornsley has control of Nyles's money.''

"Bet that rankles a bit,'' Mrs. Goodge interjected. "It's always one or the other. Women or money. Looks like in Hornsley's case, it were both.''

"And that's not all,'' Smythe continued. "Two days ago, Peter give Nyles orders not to see this Madeline Wynn again. Nyles supposedly told him to go to the devil and that he'd see his sweetheart whenever he wanted. The footman I talked to overheard Nyles threatening to kill Peter if Peter didn't let up on the purse strings so that Nyles and Madeline Wynn could get married.''

"That certainly sounds like a good reason for hatin' someone enough to kill,'' Luty put in.

"Does Nyles Hornsley have an alibi?'' Hatchet asked.

Smythe shook his head. "I don't know. He weren't at home on the evening of the murder, the footman knew that much. But that doesn't mean Nyles weren't somewhere else.''

"Are you going to pursue that line of investigation tomorrow?'' Mrs. Jeffries asked.

"If it's all the same to you,'' Smythe said smoothly. Checking up on Nyles Hornsley's alibi shouldn't take long, he thought. That would leave him plenty of time free to set Blimpey on Skegit's trail.

"I think that's a splendid idea,'' said Mrs. Jeffries as she pursed her lips. "Oh, this is so wretched,'' she cried. "If Inspector Witherspoon were on the case, we wouldn't have to be running about trying to see if someone had an alibi in the first place. We could already know! At least with our inspector, we had access to what the suspects have told the police about their whereabouts at the time of the murder.''

''Now, now, Hepzibah.'' Luty patted the housekeeper's hand. ''Don't get all het up. We've got to do what we've got to do. The inspector bein' off the case makes it a bit harder, but it ain't impossible.''

''I know.'' She sighed. ''It's just that I've got such an awful feeling about this case. The whole idea that someone would use the inspector's name and then commit murder . . .''

''I think I've figured out why,'' Smythe interrupted.

Everyone stared at him.

''Why what?'' Wiggins asked.

''Why he used the inspector's name,'' the coachman explained. ''It's dead simple once you think about it. To begin with, the inspector gets his name in the paper every time he solves a murder. If I was a killer lookin' to get into a buildin' and strangle someone, what better name to use?''

''And secondly,'' Mrs. Jeffries prompted. She too had an idea as to why the killer was using Witherspoon's name, but she wanted to learn whether the coachman had come to the same conclusion she had.

''Well, we don't know much about this Hornsley person, and what little we do know makes me believe that he weren't a very nice man,'' Smythe said slowly, his idea forming and taking shape as he spoke. ''Seems to me he might have been the kinda bloke that was on his guard. Maybe whoever killed him needed to pretend to be a policeman so he could get close enough to kill him, if you get my meanin'.''

Mrs. Jeffries nodded thoughtfully. She hadn't thought

quite along those lines, but she rather admired Smythe's reasoning. "Yes, I rather think I do. You're saying that the victim had so many enemies he might have been on his guard should a strange man have tried to get into his office after hours. The one person who he would have allowed in and turned his back on with no sense of danger would have had to have been a policeman—right?"

Smythe grinned. "Somethin' like that."

"How long do you think he's been dead?" Inspector Nivens asked the police surgeon.

"I wouldn't care to guess," Dr. Potter snapped. "Not until I've done the postmortem."

Barnes smiled in the darkness. Same old Potter. Still wouldn't tell you the sun had come up unless he'd looked out and seen it for himself. Beside him, he heard Nivens snort in disgust.

"But you must be able to tell us something," Nivens pressed. He shuffled his feet to keep warm.

"The man's dead, strangled by the look of it," Potter said irritably. "That's all I'm going to say at the moment."

"The body's still warm, sir," Barnes said softly. "I'd reckon he couldn't have been killed more than a couple of hours ago."

"And where did you take your medical degree?" Potter asked. He stood up. In the dim light cast by the policeman's lamps, he glared at the constable.

"Beggin' your pardon, sir," Barnes said to the doctor, "but I have seen a few bodies in my time on the force."

Nivens ignored them both. He pulled his pocket watch from his coat and checked the time. "It's almost nine," he mumbled. "Which means death probably occurred around seven."

Potter, incensed that the inspector was actually listening to a uniformed man, glared at both of them and scurried away. "I'll do the postmortem tomorrow," he called. "Until then make no assumptions, Inspector."

Barnes sighed. He watched Nivens bend down and start searching the pockets of the late George Frampton. Bad luck, the poor bloke had got it just like the other one. He even had a note pinned to his chest. Not that it made much sense, but it was a clue all the same.

The note had been printed on the same kind of paper and the word VIDI had been printed on it. Barnes had no idea what it meant. For that matter, neither did Inspector Nivens.

Small clusters of uniformed police were everywhere, keeping the curious away from the body and vainly trying to search the area in the dark and fog. Nivens had sent several lads off to see if they could find any witnesses, but Barnes was willing to bet his next hot dinner that they'd find no one.

This killer was too careful, too cunning. By some means, he lured his victim into a deserted park on a dark and foggy night, insuring that no one else would be larking about and then he'd struck. Stunning first and then dragging the poor bloke behind a bush to finish him off.

Made Barnes half sick, it did. He turned his gaze away from the late George Frampton. What made him even sicker was that whoever had done it was probably going to get away with it. With Nivens investigating the crime, the murderer didn't have to worry about getting caught.

"I've found something," Nivens called. "Barnes, grab that lamp and hold it closer."

Barnes did as he was told. He stepped around the fallen man's legs and held the lamp up. Nivens was holding up a plain white envelope. He opened it and drew out a piece of paper. "I found this in the victim's inside coat pocket," he said. "Hold the lamp closer, I can't quite make this out."

Barnes bent closer, bringing the lamp to within inches of Nivens's skull. He heard the inspector gasp in surprise. "What is it, sir?"

"It's a note," Nivens said, his voice rising excitedly. "And it says, *If you want to know who murdered your partner, be at the Black Horse tonight at six o'clock.*'"

"Is it signed, sir?" Barnes had a sinking feeling in the pit of his stomach and it had nothing to do with the fact that he'd not had dinner.

Nivens laughed nastily. "It's signed alright, Constable. By none other than Gerald Witherspoon!"

Mrs. Jeffries poured the inspector a cup of tea and placed it next to his plate of bacon and eggs. "How was your walk last night, sir?" she asked. She took her own tea and sat down.

"My what?" Witherspoon said, looking puzzled.

"Your walk, sir," she repeated.

"Oh yes, well, I had a jolly good walk. Went quite a long ways."

"You were gone a time, sir," she replied. "We were beginning to get worried. You didn't get in till quite late."

"Hardly late, Mrs. Jeffries," he chided. "I was home by nine."

"You looked quite winded when you came in," she persisted. "I do hope you're not overdoing things. Moderate exercise is all well and good, sir. But too much can't be good for you." She didn't think he'd been out walking, but one could hardly accuse one's employer of lying.

"I think it did me the world of good," he replied. "As I said, I walked a long way. Felt wonderful when I got home. I slept like a baby."

Betsy stuck her head in the dining room. "Constable Barnes is here to see the inspector," she announced. "Should I show him in?"

"Oh, yes," Witherspoon replied eagerly. "Mrs. Jeffries, pour another cup."

Barnes appeared a few moments later, smiled at the housemaid and nodded at Mrs. Jeffries. "Mornin', ma'am. Sir."

"Do sit down and have some tea," said Witherspoon as he gestured to the chair on his left.

"Thank you, sir," Barnes replied. His words were polite enough, but Mrs. Jeffries could tell by his expression and the way he carried himself that something was terribly wrong.

"What brings you here so early this morning?" Witherspoon asked cheerfully. "Not that I'm not delighted to see you, of course."

"I'm afraid I've got some bad news," Barnes interrupted.

Witherspoon and Mrs. Jeffries stared at him.

"George Frampton was found murdered in Hyde Park last night," the constable blurted.

"Was he killed the same way as the other victim?" Witherspoon asked.

Barnes nodded. "Coshed on the head and strangled. There was a note pinned to his chest too, just like Hornsley. Course it didn't make any sense."

"What did it say?" the inspector prodded.

"It didn't say anything," Barnes replied. "Just had VIDI printed on it. Doesn't mean anything. Doesn't make any sense at all."

Mrs. Jeffries simply could not stop herself. "What was he strangled with?"

Barnes looked over and stared at her for a long moment. Finally, he said, "A school tie."

"Just like Mr. Hornsley," she murmured.

"Any idea when he was killed?" Witherspoon asked urgently. He knew this wasn't his case, but dash it all, he couldn't stop himself from asking questions.

Barnes laughed. "Potter was the police surgeon on duty last night," he said, "so he wouldn't tell us anything. But we had a bit of luck. The body was discovered fairly soon after the murder."

"Who discovered it?" Oh well, Mrs. Jeffries thought, in for a penny, in for a pound. The constable didn't seem to mind her asking questions.

"A policeman."

"That's a bit of luck," Witherspoon exclaimed.

"Not really, sir," Barnes said quickly. "He was out lookin' for Frampton when he found the body."

Witherspoon was puzzled. "I don't understand."

"When Mr. Frampton didn't get home by seven last night, Mrs. Frampton sent one of her footman to the Yard with a message. We started lookin' right away," Barnes explained. "That's how I happened to be there. The message from Mrs. Frampton come in just before I was fixin' to go home. So we started searching and a young constable found his body in the park just before nine o'clock."

"I say, that was jolly clever of you to search the park." Witherspoon beamed at the constable. "Whose idea was that—yours?"

Barnes shook his head. "We weren't bein' clever, sir. Mrs. Frampton told us where to look. She told the constable we sent round to take her statement that her husband usually cut through the park on his way home from work. He had a routine, he did. Frampton would stop off at the Black Horse for a drink, cut through the park to give himself a bit of exercise, and be home for dinner at seven."

Mrs. Jeffries's mind worked furiously. "I take it that Mr. Frampton hadn't varied his routine because of his partner's murder."

Barnes shrugged. "We're not sure . . ."

"Then he must not have felt he was in any danger," Mrs. Jeffries continued, unaware of the uncomfortable expression on the constable's face. "Therefore, we can conclude that Frampton felt that Hornsley's murder had nothing to do with him."

"I don't think I quite follow you," Witherspoon said.

"But, sir," Mrs. Jeffries said earnestly, "I'm merely using the kind of reasoning you always use when you're on a case."

"Oh, yes," the inspector smiled. "Do go on. I'm, er, curious to see how you've applied my methods."

"Frampton wasn't a fool," she continued. "If Hornsley was murdered because of something that had gone on with his business, then Frampton would have felt himself in danger as well and taken precautions. Apparently, he took no precautions at all. He obviously felt safe enough to walk through a deserted park on a dark, foggy night. I mean, no one in their right minds would go into Hyde Park if they thought there was someone trying to kill them."

"I'm not so sure about that," Barnes said softly. But they didn't seem to hear him.

"I don't know, Mrs. Jeffries," Witherspoon put in. "People occasionally do very foolish things. Frampton's going into the park could just as easily mean he was one of those stubborn fellows who won't change their routine for anyone, certainly not for a murderer."

"Er, Inspector," Barnes said softly. "Frampton was scared. We already know that."

"He was?" Witherspoon said in surprise.

"Yes, sir," Barnes cleared his throat. "His clerk told us that Frampton was real nervous. You see, sir, he didn't go into that park alone."

Mrs. Jeffries felt a cold, hard hand clutch her heart. "Who did he go in with?"

Barnes fiddled with the handle of his teacup; he couldn't meet her gaze. "He went in with a fellow he'd met in the Black Horse. The publican overheard them talking."

Even the inspector knew something was wrong. "And did the publican happen to get this man's name?"

Barnes finally looked up. "Yes, sir. The man introduced himself as Gerald Witherspoon."

For a moment none of them said a word.

"Oh, dear," Witherspoon broke the awkward silence. "This is most odd. I was nowhere near Hyde Park or the Black Horse Pub last night. Did the publican say what the fellow looked like?"

"He had spectacles . . ."

"Oh dear," the inspector murmured.

"A bowler hat."

"Just like mine, I suppose."

"And a great big heavy overcoat," finished Barnes.

"I've got a great big heavy overcoat, too," Witherspoon said morosely.

"And that's not the worst of it, sir," Barnes said.

"You mean there's more!" The inspector couldn't make heads or tails of this. How much worse could it get?

"They found another note on Frampton's body. It was in an envelope in his top pocket. It said, '*If you want to know who killed your partner, meet me at the Black Horse Pub at six o'clock.*' "

"Was the note signed?" Mrs. Jeffries asked. She already knew it was and by whom.

Barnes nodded sadly. "It was signed Gerald Witherspoon."

"That is nonsense," Witherspoon burst out. "Utter nonsense. I would never do such a silly, melodramatic thing as that. That's ridiculous. If I wanted to meet someone I'd go round to his home or ask him to come to the Yard. I certainly wouldn't send silly little schoolboy notes to lure the victim into a deserted park!"

"Of course you wouldn't, sir," Barnes said soothingly. "Everyone knows you wouldn't do such a silly thing."

"But I have a feeling that there are some who do think I'm quite capable of such stupidity."

Barnes shook his head. "No one seriously considers you a suspect, sir. If that's what you're thinkin'. Even Nivens knows you've no reason to want to kill either Hornsley or Frampton."

Reason or not, Mrs. Jeffries knew that things were getting very bad for their inspector. Very bad, indeed. "Reasons for murder can be manufactured," she said softly. "Just as easily as a mysterious note found in a dead man's pocket."

"What?" Witherspoon looked at her curiously. The expression on his face indicated that he hoped he hadn't understood her clearly.

"Someone," she said bluntly, "is trying their hardest to make sure Inspector Witherspoon is arrested for these crimes. That person will, no doubt, manufacture a suitable motive at the appropriate time. A motive, I feel, that even someone as abysmally stupid as Inspector Nivens can't fail to see."

"Why, Mrs. Jeffries," said Witherspoon, deeply shocked. "Who would do such a wicked thing? And why to me?"

"There's lots that would do it," Barnes answered. "And especially to you. You're a good man, Inspector, but there's plenty of criminals that you've sent to prison. This could be someone's idea of the perfect revenge."

"But Inspector Nivens wouldn't arrest me," Witherspoon protested. "Surely he'd see that I was being made to look like the killer?"

"Nivens would arrest you in two shakes of dog's tail," Barnes interrupted. "He'll be here this mornin' to see if you have an alibi for last night between the hours of six and seven-thirty. But that's fine, once Nivens knows you were here at home and that your staff can confirm . . ." but he broke off when he saw their expressions change.

"I'm afraid I wasn't here at that time," the inspector admitted. "I was . . . uh . . . out walking. I didn't get home till almost nine."

"You were out takin' a ruddy walk!" Barnes stared at him incredulously. "Did anyone see you? Did you stop anywhere, have a drink or bite to eat? Did you run into any of the lads? For God's sake, man, where did you go?"

"That's just it, I didn't go anywhere. I just walked. No one saw me." Witherspoon slumped in his chair. "I'm afraid I just wandered around. To be perfectly truthful, I've been a bit upset about that first murder. You'd be upset too if someone used your name to kill a man. So I wasn't paying attention to where I was going. I was just walking and thinking."

"But did you stop anywhere?" Barnes asked hopefully. "Anywhere at all?"

"No. I wasn't hungry and I didn't stop for a drink, either. Nor did I run into any uniformed lads. I'm sorry. I saw no one."

Barnes closed his eyes. For a long moment he couldn't find his voice. Finally, he said, "Oh Lord, sir, let's hope Mrs. Jeffries is wrong."

"I'm praying I'm wrong," Mrs. Jeffries interjected. But neither Barnes nor the inspector appeared to hear her.

"Let's hope that this killer isn't deliberately trying to get you arrested for these murders," the constable continued sadly. " 'Cause if he is, you're done for."

"No, he isn't," Mrs. Jeffries announced calmly.

Both of the men stared at her. She smiled serenely. She was going to take a big gamble here—there was no choice.

If she didn't act, if she didn't take this step, there was a good chance that Inspector Gerald Witherspoon would be arrested for murder. She could feel it in her bones. Mrs. Jeffries had learned to trust her instincts, and right now they were screaming at her that Inspector Witherspoon was in peril. If not his life, then at least his reputation was at stake.

No matter what the risk, she couldn't allow him to be arrested for a crime she knew he didn't commit. If Inspector Witherspoon couldn't see the danger he was in, she had to do it for him.

"What do you mean?" Barnes asked. "I don't see that there's much we can do. Not with that nitwit Nivens investigatin' this case." He laughed bitterly. "Take my word for it, he'll never catch the real killer."

"Of course he won't," Mrs. Jeffries said calmly. "But we will."

CHAPTER 6

"Have you taken leave of your senses?" Mrs. Goodge asked incredulously. She stared at the housekeeper over the rim of her spectacles.

"Cor blimey, Mrs. J.," Smythe added. "I don't like the sound of this."

"Hell's bells, Hepzibah," Luty snapped. "I thought the whole idea was to keep our activities *secret* from the inspector."

Wiggins gaped at her in shock. Betsy groaned. Hatchet's mouth was pursed in a disapproving frown, and even Fred seemed to be looking at her as though she'd just lost her mind.

Mrs. Jeffries held up her hand. "If you'll all give me a moment to explain," she began for the third time, "I think you'll see that I had no choice whatsoever in the matter. I had to do something."

"No choice," Betsy bleated. "What does that mean?"

Mrs. Jeffries tried again. "It means that we've got to do

this case differently. Now, if you'll all calm down and let me tell you what happened, I think you'll find there is absolutely no reason to panic. The inspector has no idea we've been helping him on all his previous cases, he only thinks we're going to help on this one.''

They started talking again.

Hatchet banged his fist on the table. ''I think we owe Mrs. Jeffries the courtesy of listening to what she has to say,'' he said loudly.

Everyone fell silent, even Luty, who contented herself with giving him a quick frown. Hatchet smiled slightly, reminding Mrs. Jeffries of a schoolmaster who'd settled down a roomful of boisterous children. ''Now, madam''— he nodded at her—''do continue. I assure you'll we'll not interrupt you again.''

''Thank you, Hatchet,'' she replied. She took a deep breath. The truth was, she wasn't sure if she was doing the right thing, but she still didn't see that she'd had any choice in the matter. ''First of all, do keep in mind that the inspector has no idea we've helped him in the past.''

''Then why is 'e lettin' us investigate this one?'' Smythe asked.

''Because he has no choice,'' Mrs. Jeffries said quickly. She told them about everything she'd learned from Constable Barnes, taking care not to leave out any of the details. When she got to the part about the note with Witherspoon's signature being found in the dead man's pocket, there were gasps of shock and surprise around the table.

''So you see,'' she finished, when they'd all quieted down again. ''I had to do something. We can't let our inspector get arrested for murder.''

"Do you think there's a chance that's going to happen?" Betsy asked anxiously.

"Not if we're as clever as I think we are," Mrs. Jeffries replied. "But we need to know what the police know. For that we need Constable Barnes. We can't keep muddling about in the dark, so to speak. Inspector Witherspoon's reputation and possibly even his liberty are at grave risk. There's a chance we'll miss something important if we try and do this one completely on our own."

Smythe shook his head in disgust. "Nivens has always looked down 'is nose at Inspector Witherspoon, but I can't believe he'd arrest 'im for murder."

"Nivens is desperate to solve this case," Mrs. Jeffries pointed out. "And this killer is very, very clever. The real danger isn't our inspector getting arrested on such flimsy evidence. It's giving the killer a chance to plant the kind of evidence that will force Nivens to arrest Inspector Witherspoon."

"You're assuming the killer is deliberately making it look as if Witherspoon is guilty?" Hatchet said slowly, his face creased in a thoughtful frown.

"We'd be fools to assume otherwise," Mrs. Jeffries replied. "The killer used Witherspoon's name twice to gain access to his victims. What's worse, he's actually planted evidence on George Frampton that points blame directly at our inspector."

Smythe leaned forward, resting his elbows on the table. "Then that means it's got to be someone who's got it in for Inspector Witherspoon," he said.

"I think that's a fairly safe assumption."

"Could it be someone he's arrested in the past?" Luty queried.

"I'm not sure," Mrs. Jeffries hesitated. "Before he started solving homicides, he spent most of his career with the police in the records room. Yet"—she paused and thought for a moment, then she shook her head—"I can't think of anyone he's arrested for murder who's at liberty now."

"Most of 'em are either 'anged or doin' time," Smythe mused. "So maybe it's someone's relation? You know, I mean it could be a brother or a cousin or even a friend of someone the inspector arrested."

"Well, whoever it is," Mrs. Jeffries said, "is keen and very daring. We've no time to lose."

Betsy's brows drew together in a puzzled frown. "There's somethin' I don't understand. Are we goin' under the assumption that it's the inspector the killer is really after? I mean, gettin' him arrested for murder and ruining his career? Or is the killer really wantin' the victims dead and out of his way?"

Mrs. Jeffries had pondered that question too. "Unfortunately, I don't have an answer for you. At this point, we simply don't know," she said, shrugging her shoulders helplessly. "But there are two people dead. I don't think the killer picked them arbitrarily. Let's assume that for reasons that aren't clear yet, the murderer also wants certain other people, mainly those he's already murdered, out of the way."

"Killing two birds with one stone, so to speak," Wiggins smiled at his own wit.

"That's an excellent way of putting it," Mrs. Jeffries

said to the footman; she was delighted to see that he wasn't sulking anymore.

"What do we do now?" Betsy asked. "Continue as we are? Or should one of us hang about here and keep an eye on the inspector?"

Mrs. Jeffries thought for a moment. "There's no need to do that. I don't think Inspector Witherspoon is in any immediate danger. But, I do think we ought to shift the focus of this investigation."

"Shift it how?" Mrs. Goodge asked.

"I'm not exactly sure. It's more complex than we first thought," she replied slowly. She was thinking aloud, hoping that something she said would spark some ideas in the others. "Perhaps we ought to spend more time concentrating on the firm of Hornsley, Frampton, and Whitelaw? Oh dear, I'm not explaining this very well, but since Frampton was the second person killed, I suspect that the murders have more to do with the victims' business lives than with their personal lives."

"So what do ya want us to do?" Smythe asked.

"Well, I'd like you to learn what you can about Grady Whitelaw," she said. "He's the last of the partners left."

The coachman nodded. "Alright, I'll get onto 'im today."

"What about me?" Betsy asked.

"You take Justin Vincent, the silent partner," Mrs. Jeffries instructed. "Find out what you can about him."

"I take it you want Madam and me to continue using our sources in the City to learn what we can about the firm," Hatchet said.

"That's right," Mrs. Jeffries replied. "But don't ignore

116   Emily Brightwell

your gossip sources either," she said, smiling at Luty. "Your friend Myrtle seems a very fountain of information."

Luty chuckled. "Oh, don't worry, Hepzibah, I won't be forgettin' Myrtle. She knows more about the people with money in this city than the Queen's tax boys."

"What about me?" Mrs. Goodge asked. "My sources won't know much about the goings on of the firm, so what am I supposed to do?"

"What you always do," Mrs. Jeffries said firmly. She wasn't going to have the cook feeling left out and unimportant. "Even a business firm has a past. I've every confidence you can find out a great deal of useful information. Besides, we're not going to totally ignore the victims' personal lives, so find out what more you can about that, too."

"I guess Fred and me won't have nuthin' to do again," Wiggins complained. He shot his bandaged ankle a fierce glare. " 'Ow long is this ruddy thing goin' to take before it 'eals?"

Mrs. Jeffries gazed at him sympathetically. In truth, she still couldn't think of a thing that poor Wiggins could do. "I know it's difficult," she began, "but there's really nothing you can do right now. You must give yourself time to heal. It would be far too dangerous for you to try and go out and about in your condition. We can't have you hurting yourself."

"Don't worry, lad," Smythe said kindly, "that ankle won't take forever to 'eal. You'll be out and about on the next case."

"If there is a next case," Wiggins muttered.

"Remember everyone," Mrs. Jeffries said, "Constable

Barnes is coming by tonight after supper to give us a progress report. So let's all try to have something to contribute.''

Hatchet cleared his throat. ''Does the inspector know that Madam and I are helping?''

''No,'' Mrs. Jeffries replied, ''he doesn't. I thought it best not to mention your participation.''

''Then perhaps Madam and I ought to drop by after you've had your meeting with Constable Barnes,'' Hatchet suggested.

''That's a good idea,'' she said, relieved that neither Luty nor her butler had taken offense. ''Shall we say half past nine?''

''I've no idea why anyone would want to kill George or Peter,'' Grady Whitelaw said to the two policemen. ''No idea at all.''

Whitelaw was a thin, nervous man with receding brown hair, bushy eyebrows, and crooked nose. Though it was only nine in the morning, his pristine white shirt was rumpled, his expensive black coat was wrinkled and creased, and his tie askew.

Barnes thought Whitelaw was the most fidgety creature he'd ever seen. They'd only been in the room two minutes and the man hadn't been still a moment. His hands fluttered, his shoulders jerked spasmodically, and he'd jumped up from his chair at least twice. Barnes cast a quick look at the other man in Whitelaw's office—Justin Vincent, the silent partner.

Vincent was about the same age as Whitelaw, but that was the only thing they had in common. His hair was light brown and his face clean shaven. He sat in the chair to one side of Whitelaw's desk, his brown eyes reflecting confidence and good humor. He was tall, dressed in a dark brown suit with fawn-colored gloves, and, most of all, calm.

"Of course Peter was a blighter," Whitelaw rattled on, fluttering his hands like he was batting at flies. "Always has been, even when we were in school. Made the younger boys miserable."

Barnes saw Vincent wince. He didn't much blame the man. If Whitelaw didn't pause to take a breath, he was going to work himself into a fit. It was bloomin' embarrassin' to watch.

"But George was a decent sort," Whitelaw cried. He ran a hand through his hair, causing it to stand straight up. "Why would anyone want to kill George?"

"That's what we're going to find out," Inspector Nivens replied.

"Yes, but *when* are you going to find out?"

Nivens ignored that question. "Do you know if either man had received any threatening letters?"

Barnes stifled a sigh. Nivens was at it again. Why didn't the man ask something useful? Why didn't he ask them about their alibis? Why didn't he ask them about the notes pinned to the dead men's coats? Bloody fool.

"Threatening letters?" Whitelaw repeated. His pale face creased in thought as he contemplated it. "I don't think so. Neither of them ever mentioned it if they did."

"Do you know of anyone who'd want to ruin your firm?" Nivens asked.

"Of course not," Whitelaw exclaimed.

"But I understand some of your competitors don't like the way you conduct business," Nivens said.

"*Most* of our competitors don't like the way we do business." Whitelaw shrugged, but it wasn't a simple movement. His whole body shook as his head bobbed and his shoulders shot up so high that Barnes was amazed that he stayed in his chair.

"But that's hardly a reason for murder," Whitelaw's voice cracked. "We've been doing business this way for years."

"What about Damon Hilliard?" Nivens pressed. "Does he like the way you operate?"

"Hilliard's complained about our tactics for years," Whitelaw replied. "We don't pay much attention to him."

"Wasn't he in here a few days ago, the day that Peter Hornsley was murdered?" Nivens said. "And didn't he threaten him?"

"Oh, no."

"No?" Nivens repeated in surprise. "But we've had it on good authority . . ."

"Hilliard threatened Peter a few days before Peter was killed," Whitelaw corrected. "But we didn't take it seriously. It wasn't the first time it had happened. He's a bad temper, but I don't think he's a murderer."

Nivens opened his mouth but before he could get a word out, Vincent interrupted. "Excuse me, Inspector, but do the police seriously think these murders were done by someone with a grudge against the firm?"

"We think it's possible, sir," Nivens replied.

"How long have you been associated with the company?" Barnes asked Vincent. He didn't much care whether or not Nivens liked his asking questions. He wasn't going to stand by and let a killer walk free because of his superior's incompetence.

"I bought into the firm several months ago." Vincent smiled.

"Had you known either of the victims previous to your buying in, sir?" Barnes pressed.

"Oh no," Vincent laughed easily. "I haven't been in England long enough to know many people. I only came over from America a few months ago."

"And how did you happen to invest money in Hornsley, Frampton, and Whitelaw?"

"I can answer that," Whitelaw interrupted. "I ran into Justin at my club. We were introduced by a mutual acquaintance. He was looking to invest some capital, and I thought, why not us? We're a safe investment."

"So you bought in as a silent partner?" Barnes probed.

Beside him, Nivens cleared his throat. "That'll be all, Constable. I don't think Mr. Vincent's business dealings have any connection to this matter."

"As you wish, sir." He forced himself to smile. "But I do believe we've forgotten to ask these gentlemen where they were last night between six and half past seven."

Nivens's eyes widened at the constable's audacity. But for form's sake, he couldn't make an issue out of the statement. "Gentlemen," he said, "if you'd be so kind as to answer the constable's inquiry."

"I was at my fiancée's home," Whitelaw replied.

"What time did you arrive there, sir?" Barnes asked quickly.

"About eight-fifteen, I think."

"So you left your office quite late?"

"Oh no, I left at my usual time," Whitelaw explained. "Half past five. George was still here when I went. I popped my head into his office to say good night," he sniffed.

"And it took you three hours to get to your fiancée's?" Barnes asked incredulously. "Where does she live?"

Whitelaw wiped his eyes. "She lives near Regent's Park, but I went home first and changed clothes. Then I got a hansom, but there was a dreadful amount of traffic. It took ages to get to her home. She was most annoyed with me for being late."

Barnes turned to Vincent. "And you, sir, where were you last night?"

"I'm afraid I've no alibi, either," Vincent said. "My servants were home but I was shut in my study working. I didn't see anyone after, oh . . ." he paused for a moment. "I guess it must have been half-past six."

"Didn't you eat an evening meal?" Nivens asked.

"I'm afraid I've taken on a number of habits from my adopted country," he said, smiling broadly. "Americans tend to eat earlier than we do. I had my meal at six."

"I don't see why you're asking us all these questions," Whitelaw suddenly cried.

"It's our duty to ask you these questions," Nivens said pompously. "A murder had been committed."

Whitelaw's eyes narrowed angrily. "I'm aware there's been a murder. Two of them, in fact. But instead of wasting time badgering me, you'd do better asking those that are going to benefit from my friend's death where they were last night."

"Whom do you mean, sir?" Barnes queried softly.

"Ask Stuart Frampton where he was last night when his father was being murdered," said Whitelaw, his head bobbing wildly in excitement, his face flushed a bright red. "After all, now that George is gone, Stuart gets it all."

"Is that where you work, then?" Betsy asked the young woman she'd been walking with. They were in front of a lovely red brick house in Mayfair.

"This is the place. Lovely i'n' it?" Martha Dowling said eagerly, obviously taking pride in working in so grand a house. She was a tall, big-boned girl in her early twenties with light brown hair tucked neatly under a maid's cap. Her face was round and her complexion almost perfect. Betsy thought she had the loveliest hazel eyes. "I've been there for three months now," she continued. "I used to work for a solicitor and his family over on Bulstrode Street, but I come here when me mum saw an advert in the newspaper. It's much better here. Mr. Vincent don't work his servants like they was dogs."

"And he lets you out every now and again," Betsy said, giving the girl a cheerful smile. "That's always nice, too."

"Well, there's always errands that need doin' and such like that," Martha agreed. "Mr. Vincent doesn't have a butler, just a housekeeper. She's not one for running about and such. Like this morning, for instance, Mrs. Tottle didn't want to have to take Mr. Vincent's boots to the shoemaker, so she let me do it. I like gettin' out."

Betsy nodded. "I suppose Mr. Vincent has lived here a long time," she mused. Martha didn't seem to be in a hurry to get inside and start scrubbing floors, not that Betsy could blame the girl. Housework was about the most boring thing a body could do.

Martha shook her head and leaned against the wrought-iron fence in front of the house. "Mr. Vincent only come here a few months back. He's from America, you know. He once worked in a traveling show. Can you imagine that?"

"But this house is so big," Betsy said, feigning amazement. "I thought he must be someone from one of them old rich families. You know, the kind that are always braggin' and sayin' things like their ancestors come over with the conqueror."

Martha laughed. "Mr. Vincent's not at all like that. Not that he's isn't rich as sin, he is. But he's only lived here a few months."

"You mean he's a foreigner!"

"He's as English as the Queen," Martha replied. "Went to school in Abingdon. But he's lived in America for years. Somewhere out in California . . ." She broke off, her eyes taking on a dreamy glazed expression. "I've always wanted to go to California. Mr. Vincent says the sun settin' in the Pacific Ocean is one of the most beautiful sights in the world. He's fixin' to go back soon. I wish he'd take me with 'im."

"You like 'im then?"

Martha gave her a sharp look. "I like workin' for him. He's not so fussy as some are, if you get my meaning."

"Pays well and keeps his hands to himself," Betsy stated.

Martha grinned knowingly. "That's right. I'd rather work for the likes of him than for some I've known."

Betsy knew she had to find out where Justin Vincent was on the evening of the murders. She hoped the man wasn't the killer. Vincent sounded much nicer than most of the employers in London. But justice was justice. Because a man treated his servants well didn't mean he wasn't capable of coshing someone over the head and strangling the life out of them.

But Betsy had to go carefully. Martha seemed a right chatty, trusting sort of girl, but she wasn't stupid. Betsy didn't want to ask too much. "Is he married?"

"No." Martha sighed. "And it's a right shame, too. He's such a nice man and not bad lookin' for his age. I think he had his heart broken when he was a lad, if you know what I mean."

"Really?"

"Oh, yes," Martha continued. "Sometimes I see him sittin' in his big wingbacked chair in front of the fireplace. He'll have the saddest expression on his face. And one time, I was bringing some fresh towels into his bedroom, and I saw him bent over this old carpetbag he keeps under his bed and you'll never guess what he was holdin'."

"What?"

"A lock of a woman's hair." Martha's hazel eyes widened dramatically. "I think it must have belonged to his sweetheart." She sighed again. "It's so sad. He could do with a bit of softness in his life. Oh well, maybe he's got someone waitin' for him in California."

"Doesn't he ever go out?"

"Not much." Martha made a face. "If I had his money, I'd be out every night. But all he ever does is shut himself up in the study after supper and work."

"I suppose he makes you all bring him tea and coffee while he's workin' them late hours," Betsy said disgustedly, as though she was very familiar with inconsiderate employers.

"Nah," said Martha, pushing away from the fence and straightening her spine. "He doesn't like to be bothered after supper. He doesn't even have a servant to help him get ready for bed. Like I said, he's a good master."

Betsy felt like pulling her hair out. Martha was giving her lots of information, but she couldn't for the life of her think of a way to find out if Vincent had been out on the night of the murders. Out of the corner of her eye, she saw a tall, white-haired man getting out of a carriage in the street ahead of her. It gave her an idea.

"Is Mr. Vincent a tall, dark-haired gentleman?" she asked Martha. "I was up on the High Street last night, and I saw a man like that having an argument with a cabbie." She forced herself to laugh. "I thought they was goin' to come to blows."

"I don't think so," Martha said slowly, her face creased in thought. "Mr. Vincent's got light brown hair and he's not all that tall. More medium height like. But he's not the sort to be gettin' into fights. What time was it?"

"Around seven o'clock," Betsy replied. "I was on my way home. My employer insists we've got to be in by nine even on our day out."

"Then it couldn't have been Mr. Vincent," Martha said firmly. "He was shut in his study from half-past six on. He's done that every night for the past couple of weeks."

That's all Betsy needed to know. She smiled at Martha, chatted a few minutes more and told her new friend she had to go. Martha gave her a friendly wave and went into the house.

Betsy's shoulders slumped as she went back up to the main road. It was bloomin' hard to concentrate. Even when she'd been talking with Martha and tryin' her very best to keep her mind on this case, she'd not been able to stop thinking about Raymond Skegit. Why did he have to show up now?

She rounded the corner and almost bumped into an elegantly dressed woman. Betsy gave her an apologetic smile and dodged round her ample bulk. Blast a Spaniard, as Smythe would say, she didn't want the likes of Raymond hanging about and ruining her life. The truth was, she was scared of Raymond. There'd been stories about him, ugly stories.

But there was nothing she could do but be on her guard. Make sure she didn't put herself in a situation where Raymond could get his dirty hands on her again. She'd have to be careful. Betsy stepped off the curb into the street. Immediately, the air was filled with the squeal of brakes and the sound of horses' hooves.

"Hey, girl," an angry cooper's driver screamed, "watch where yer goin'."

She leapt back out of harm's way and waited for the dray to pass. Blast, blast, blast, she cursed silently to herself. This was awful. She was so rattled she'd be lucky to get home without being killed. And to make matters worse, she'd been so upset yesterday evening, she hadn't even told the others what she'd learned.

And what was she goin' to do about Smythe? She looked around her quickly just to make sure he wasn't hangin'

about. Not that she'd mind him hangin' about. He'd come
in right handy when Raymond was tryin' to drag her off
yesterday, but she didn't want him spyin' on her all the
time. She sighed and crossed the road. What was she goin'
to do? What if Smythe found out? Oh Lord, why did this
have to happen now, just when she and the coachman were
really gettin' to know each other.

She liked Smythe. Really liked him. Recently, she'd had
hopes that maybe, if she was real lucky like, the two of
them could have something more than just a friendship. But
if he found out about her past, he'd want nothing to do
with her. Smythe was a good man, but he was still a man.
Blast a Spaniard! It just wasn't fair.

"I'm sorry to have to bother you at a time like this," Nivens said softly. He gave Rosalind Frampton a sympathetic
smile. "But we really must ask you a few questions."

Rosalind Frampton was dark-haired, dainty, and very
beautiful. She was also a great deal younger than her late
husband.

She smiled weakly at Nivens and fiddled with the black
bombazine fabric of her mourning skirt. "I understand.
Poor George was murdered . . ." Her voice broke and she
looked away.

Barnes shuffled his feet. Bloomin' awkward this was, a
weeping widow and dozens of questions that needed answering. Thank God Inspector Witherspoon was willing to
snoop about some on this case. Barnes smiled slightly,
thinking of Witherspoon's housekeeper and her daring offer
to have the inspector's servants take a hand in as well. It
couldn't hurt, Barnes thought, shooting Nivens a disgusted

glance. He just wanted this case solved so he could go back to working with Inspector Witherspoon. He knew how to treat his constable properly.

"Would you tell us the sequence of events that led you to send for the police last night?" Nivens asked.

Rosalind Frampton looked confused. "Sequence of events," she repeated. "You mean, why did I send the footman to Scotland Yard when George didn't come home last night?"

"That's correct."

"Because he didn't come home," she explained. "George is always home by seven o'clock. You can set the clock by his coming in the front door. When it had gone seven fifteen, I knew something was wrong."

"You were alarmed?"

"I was terrified," she said, looking at Nivens as though he were thick as two short planks. "There had been another murder, if you'll remember. Peter Hornsley isn't even buried yet. Of course I was worried. So I sent Chandler, that's the footman, out with a message for the police. A few hours later, they came and told me George was dead."

"I see." Nivens bobbed his head. "Did your husband have any enemies?"

Barnes gritted his teeth. Not that again.

"Enemies?" Rosalind repeated the word like she'd never heard it before. "I don't know what you mean."

"He means," said a voice from the door, "did someone hate him enough to want to kill him."

Barnes turned and saw a dark-haired youth who looked to be in his early twenties leaning against the frame of the double doors. The young man smiled slightly when he saw he had the attention of everyone in the room.

"I'm Stuart Frampton," he announced. "George Frampton's son." He cast a quick cold look at his stepmother. "You really should have let me know the police were here."

"Why?" the look she gave him was equally cold. "They didn't ask to speak to you."

"Mr. Frampton," Nivens interrupted. "Do you know if your father was in fear of his life?"

Stuart shrugged and ambled to the settee. He perched on the arm. "He was frightened. But I don't think that's particularly odd. He had good reason to be. After all, his partner had just been murdered. He didn't have much faith in you lot, either. Said you hadn't a prayer in catching this killer."

Nivens's expression hardened. "Mr. Frampton, where were you last night between the hours of six and seven?"

"Oh," Stuart smiled cheerfully. "Am I a suspect then?"

"Just answer the question, sir."

"Did you ask my stepmother where she was?"

"I was right here," Rosalind Frampton exclaimed. "Every servant in the household can vouch for me."

"They'd say anything you want them to." Stuart glared at her. "They'll do anything to keep their positions. And even if you were here, did you tell the police where you were on the night Peter was killed?"

She gasped, outraged. "I was visiting friends that night," she sputtered. "And they can vouch for my whereabouts . . ."

"Oh, yes," he smiled slyly, "your friends. Father

wouldn't have them in the house, would he.'' He turned to the policemen. ''My stepmother used to be an actress. She's got the oddest assortment of 'friends.' Some of them quite dangerous looking. Why, I expect there's one or two that would cut your throat for half a bob.''

''That's despicable,'' Rosalind cried angrily. ''I'm not the one who benefits by George's death. You are.''

''With him dead you've got the house and an allowance and that which you wanted most, your freedom,'' Stuart yelled.

''You cur,'' Rosalind half rose from the settee. ''If you're trying to imply I had anything to do with these murders . . .''

''I'm not implying anything . . .''

''Mr. Frampton,'' Nivens cut in. ''Would you please answer the question?''

Barnes looked at his superior incredulously. For God's sake, both of them had lost their tempers and were losing control of their tongues! And Nivens had been stupid enough to interrupt. Why hadn't he kept his mouth shut? They might have learned all kinds of useful information if Nivens had let them keep on goin' at each other.

''Oh, very well,'' said Stuart, folding his arms over his chest. ''If you must know, I was at Balour's. There was a reception and concert.''

Damn, thought Barnes, half of London was at Balour's last night. ''Did anyone see you, sir?'' he asked quickly. He didn't much care that Nivens had told him to keep his mouth shut. Inspector Witherspoon's reputation, if not his life, was at stake.

''I'm sure dozens of people saw me.''

"Do you happen to know their names?" Nivens asked. He contented himself with giving Barnes a cold stare. The constable ignored it.

"If you're asking did I see anyone I know"—Stuart made a helpless gesture with his hands—"then the answer is 'no,' I didn't."

"You were there on your own, sir?" Barnes continued. "Isn't that a bit odd?"

"Not at all," Stuart replied. "I was supposed to go with some friends, the Cullens. But at the last moment, they had to cancel. You can verify that with them."

Barnes nodded slowly. "Where do the Cullens live?"

Stuart frowned. "Let's see, it's number ten Dowager Court or is it . . ."

"It's number twelve," Rosalind Frampton interjected. "And you didn't say anything to me or your father about going with the Cullens."

"I didn't consider it any of your business," Stuart shot back.

"What time did you leave?" Nivens pressed.

Barnes noticed that Rosalind Frampton had relaxed back against the settee. The ghost of a smile hovered on her mouth. She seemed to be enjoying listening to her stepson being questioned.

"It was early," Stuart replied. "Frankly, the whole thing was a bit of a bore. The music wasn't very good, the food was mediocre, and the company was hardly stimulating. I suppose I actually left at about eight o'clock."

Nivens stroked his chin; he appeared deep in thought. Finally, he asked, "Did you come straight home?"

"No," Rosalind interrupted, "he didn't." She paused

and gave her stepson a malicious smile. "Stuart didn't get in until almost ten o'clock. Not more than half an hour before the police came to tell me they'd found George's body."

CHAPTER 7

Blimpey Groggins raised his glass to his lips, took a long swallow of bitter, and then sighed in satisfaction. "Nothin' like a good drink at the end of the day to chase a man's troubles away, eh, Smythe?" He was a fat red-haired man wearing a dirty, rust-colored pork pie hat, a misshapen checkered coat spotted with grease stains, and a pristine white shirt.

Smythe stared at him for a moment, wondering how someone as filthy as Blimpey always managed to keep his shirt looking clean. The man surely enjoyed his drink too, judging by the expression on Blimpey's face. Smythe wished it were that simple for him. If pale ale or bitter was all it took to rid himself of his worries, he'd have been in the pub all day. But he wasn't much of a drinker, and he didn't think there was enough alcohol in all of England to keep him from frettin' over Betsy. "That's what some say. Look, 'ave you found out . . ."

"Now, don't be in such a 'urry, lad. I only just got 'ere.

Give me a minute to enjoy me drink before you start jumpin' down me throat with questions.'' Blimpey wiped his mouth with the cuff of his soiled sleeve.

Smythe forced himself to be patient. It didn't do any good to try and hurry Blimpey. For all the man's irritatin' ways, there was none better than Groggins at snoopin' about and learnin' what a body needed to know. ''You got my note, then,'' Smythe said casually as though the matter was of no importance.

''I'm 'ere, ain't I?'' Blimpey grinned. ''Mind you, almost didn't come when I found out what pub it was you wanted to meet in,'' he said, glancing scornfully around his surroundings.

The pub was a new one called the Brighton. There was heavy oak panelling along the walls, ornate etched glass in the windows, padded seats on the benches in the private bar, and, most bizarre of all, potted plants along the bar. Blimpey wrinkled his nose. ''Don't much 'old with these new ways of doin' things. What's wrong with nice plain walls and good hardwood floors, that's what I want to know.''

''I wanted to meet you 'ere because it was the closest pub to where I was goin' to be,'' Smythe explained. ''Besides, why do you care? The bitter here is just as good as any you'd get somewhere else.'' He really was starting to run out of patience. ''Now, 'ave you found out anything or not?''

Blimpey sighed and put his glass down. ''Don't get your trousers in a pinch,'' he mumbled. ''I've learned plenty.''

''Well,'' Smythe demanded, ''get on with it.''

''First of all, it weren't easy trackin' the likes of Raymond Skegit.'' Blimpey's cheerful countenance vanished. He looked at his companion speculatively. ''What you wantin' to know about someone like Skegit for?''

''Never mind why,'' Smythe replied impatiently. God, he'd forgotten how hard it was to actually get Blimpey to get to the point. The man did like the sound of his own voice. ''Just tell me.''

''All right, alright, keep yer shirt on.'' Blimpey cleared his throat. ''Skegit's a bad lot. Runs a string of whores out of the East End. Mind you, 'is girls is better quality than the street whores, right pretty they are and young too.'' Blimpey took a quick sip of his drink. In the weak gaslight, he didn't notice that his companion had gone pale.

''Not that runnin' whores is what makes him such a bad lot,'' Blimpey chuckled, ''there's plenty that do that. It's a way of life over in the East End. But most of 'em watch out for their girls, keep an eye on 'im and make sure they don't get knocked about by the customers. Old Jebidah Mantell even pays for his girls to go to the country once a year. Can you believe it? But nobody'd accuse Skegit of doin' something that decent. The man is different.''

''Different 'ow?'' Smythe hoped his voice sounded normal. Truth was, what he'd just heard had fair knocked the wind out of him. Of all the things he imagined, he'd never for a moment thought that Betsy could be a . . . no, he shut off that line of thought. He wasn't passin' judgment till he knew more.

''Got a mean streak, 'e does,'' Blimpey went on. ''A customer cheats one of 'is girls and Skegit'll take it out of the man's hide. But that's not the worst.''

Smythe's fingers tightened around his glass. "Go on," he ordered.

Blimpey drew closer and tossed a quick look about him to make sure no one was eavesdropping. "There's been a couple of his girls that 'ave disappeared. You know, gone. And it was always a girl who crossed him."

"Crossed 'im how? You mean like not givin' the bastard their earnin's?"

"Nah," said Blimpey, shaking his head. "Skegit would just beat 'em for that. These was girls that wanted out. One of the girls was named Molly Owens, she were only nineteen but she got tired of the trade, got 'erself a job at the Two Bulls out in Essex. Well, word 'as it that Raymond didn't much care for that. Molly was one of his best earners. Anyway, one night Molly didn't show up for work. No one ever seen 'er again."

"Cor blimey," Smythe exclaimed. "Are you sayin' he killed 'er! Just for wantin' out? Why? There's plenty of girls over in Skegit's part of town he could get to take 'er place."

"He's a mean bastard, that's why." Blimpey took another swallow. "And Skegit don't find it easy to replace girls." He smiled slyly. "Some of 'is customers 'ave, shall we say, rather peculiar tastes. He pays well, but a lot of the girls won't 'ave anything to do with 'im. Not if they 'ave any smarts."

Smythe took a drink. He was shocked all the way to his toes. This monster was someone who knew Betsy. Knew her well enough to try and drag her off.

"I've got to get goin'," Blimpey said. "Got me money?"

Smythe fumbled in his pockets, his shaking fingers grasping a roll of notes. He tossed the money on the counter. "Can you do another job for me?" he asked.

"Corse I can." The sight of all those pound notes had Blimpey's eyes shining. Smythe was a funny bloke. Tough as nails, yet there was something about him that made you think the man had a heart. Like if you was in trouble, bad trouble, you could go to him and he'd give you a hand. Mind you, the fact that the fellow weren't cheap didn't hurt none either. "What do you want?"

Smythe smiled coldly.

Blimpey drew back a little, as the expression on his companion's face sent a chill up his spine. "I mean, what else can I do for you?"

Smythe fingered another wad of notes. "I want you to find out Raymond Skegit's whereabouts."

"You mean, where 'e lives and such?" Blimpey wasn't so sure that was a good idea.

"That's right. Where 'e lives, where 'e drinks, and where 'e 'angs about."

"Smythe," Blimpey said hesitantly. "You don't want to do that. Skegit's a right bad 'un . . ."

"Let me worry about Skegit," Smythe ordered. "You just get me the information. I'll take care of the rest."

"I'm not so sure this is such a good idea," Mrs. Goodge hissed.

The staff was gathered round for their nightly meeting. But what made this one so different was that instead of being cozily ensconced in the kitchen, they were sitting stiffly around the dining room table.

Constable Barnes and the inspector were there, too.

"I say," the inspector smiled. Really, he was so very touched that his staff was willing to try and help him. Not that he actually thought they could solve this case, but at least he felt less alone. Less like his reputation was going to be torn to shreds with no one to have faith in him. He hadn't been sure he ought to let them get involved. This was police business, after all. But what harm could it do? It wasn't as if they were actually going to find out anything useful. Their hearts were in the right place, and for the world he wouldn't make light of their generous offer. But really, it wasn't as if they were actually going to catch the killer. "It's jolly good of all of you to want to help me."

"But of course we want to help you, sir," Mrs. Jeffries said stoutly. "We know you're innocent."

"Of course you are," Constable Barnes interjected.

"We wouldn't work for somebody who killed people," Mrs. Goodge declared.

"Corse we knows you didn't kill those blokes," Wiggins said around a mouth full of Battenberg cake. Smythe and Betsy shook their heads in agreement.

Mrs. Jeffries glanced at the carriage clock on the sideboard. Delighted as she was to see how the staff had rallied around Inspector Witherspoon, time was getting on. Luty and Hatchet would be here soon.

"Constable Barnes," Mrs. Jeffries said firmly, "how is the official investigation proceeding?"

Barnes smiled cynically. "Let's put it this way, if the likes of Inspector Nivens was all that stood between us and bein' murdered in our beds, then we'd best all say our prayers. The man couldn't find a bun in a bake shop, let alone solve a murder. Take today. Here we was questionin' the other partners, standing right there in the same office with Grady Whitelaw and Justin Vincent and all that Nivens could think to ask was did the victims have any enemies?'' He shook his head in disgust. ''Of course the men had enemies! They're dead, aren't they?''

''You mean he didn't ask about the notes pinned to the victims' chests?'' Mrs. Jeffries asked. Surely Barnes was exaggerating. Surely.

But he wasn't. ''Didn't say a thing about them. Every time I tried to get a few words in, askin' something useful like, Nivens would interrupt.''

Witherspoon clucked his tongue. ''Now, Barnes, we mustn't be too hard on Inspector Nivens. He's never done a murder before. Perhaps he's unsure of himself, lacks confidence, so to speak.''

''He's got enough confidence for ten men,'' Barnes shot back. ''What he lacks is thinking ability! He doesn't question any of the servants, he pretends the clerks and the staff at the victims' office are deaf, dumb, and blind, and he's so scared of offendin' someone important, he's going to let a murderer go free.'' Barnes suddenly realized he was shouting. He looked at the startled faces around the table and blushed. ''Pardon me, I didn't mean to yell like that. It's just it makes my blood boil to see him making a right old muddle of this case.''

Mrs. Jeffries understood precisely what the constable meant. ''What do you think the notes mean?''

Barnes shrugged. ''I don't rightly know. I tried asking Hornsley's staff if they had any notions about what

V-E-N-I might mean. I asked Frampton's clerks the same thing about V-I-D-I, but no one had any idea.''

''Maybe Veni has somethin' to do with Venice,'' Wiggins suggested. ''Maybe that's where the killer first met Mr. Hornsley.''

''That's a most interesting thought, Wiggins,'' said the inspector, beaming at the footman. ''Perhaps we should find out if Hornsley ever visited Venice.''

''I'll see to it tomorrow,'' Barnes said. ''Wonder what VIDI could mean?''

Mrs. Jeffries suddenly thought of something to keep Wiggins occupied. ''Why don't we let Wiggins have a go at figuring that out?'' She turned to him and asked, ''Do you think you could make your way to Mudies if I put you in a hansom tomorrow?''

''I could do it,'' Wiggins said excitedly. ''But would they let me 'ave a go at their books?'' Mudies was an excellent lending library. But he wasn't sure if they'd even let him in the door, let alone touch their precious books.

''I'll send a note along to Mr. Masters, the director,'' Mrs. Jeffries said confidently. ''I'm sure he won't mind if you do some research on the inspector's behalf.''

Wiggins's happy grin faded as he realized the enormity of the task he'd been given. ''Uh, Mrs. Jeffries, what am I supposed to find out?''

''Anything you can think of which will give us some clue as to what those notes mean.'' She smiled confidently. ''You're a smart lad. Try the atlas first.'' She didn't really expect Wiggins to come up with anything, but it would give him something to do and, more importantly, it would keep him out of Mrs. Goodge's way.

"I say, Barnes," asked Witherspoon, "did you find out anything else?"

Barnes grinned. "Despite Nivens's best efforts to the contrary, we did learn a few interestin' bits."

He told them about the remainder of the interview with Justin Vincent and Grady Whitelaw. "We got the most important information right at the end of the interview." He took a quick sip of tea. "Grady Whitelaw practically accused Stuart Frampton of murderin' his own father. Seems that now that the old man is gone, the boy gets it all."

"Gracious," Witherspoon exclaimed. "Did he really? But what about the Hornsley murder? Why would Stuart Frampton want Peter Hornsley dead?"

"That's what I wondered. But Nivens seemed to think there could be a conspiracy between Nyles Hornsley and Frampton. Each of them had a good reason to want the victims dead. Nyles so that he could marry Madeline Wynn and get his hands on the money Peter controlled, and Stuart for just about the same reason—money."

"Did either Vincent or Whitelaw have alibis for the time of the murder?" Mrs. Jeffries asked. She still thought the murders had something to do with the firm, not with the personal circumstances of the victims.

"For the Frampton killing, Whitelaw claims he was stuck in traffic, which is possible, I suppose. A dray overturned on Oxford Street and things come to a standstill for a long while. But considerin' that Frampton was killed in Hyde Park, the killer could easily have known about the traffic situation and used it to his advantage. The carriages and hansoms was backed up all the way to Hyde Park Corner."

"Has anyone asked his fiancée what time he arrived?" Betsy asked.

Barnes nodded. "I had one of the lads nip over. Miss Rawlings-Rand confirms that Whitelaw arrived at her house a little after eight."

"What about for the Hornsley murder?" Witherspoon asked.

"Whitelaw claims he was home by himself. Said he went straight home at half past five last Friday night. But we can't confirm that alibi. It was the servants' day out."

"What about Vincent?" Smythe said.

"He was at home both nights," Barnes replied. "His servants confirmed it. They've only been with him for a few months, so I don't think any of them would lie on his behalf. Seems that Vincent eats an early meal and then goes into his study to work."

"That's true," Betsy said eagerly. She blushed as everyone looked at her. "I mean, I talked to one of Vincent's maids today and she says that's what he does every night. Eats early and then goes into work."

"How very clever of you, Betsy," said Witherspoon, genuinely impressed. "Gracious, I'd no idea you could be so very resourceful."

"Thank you, sir."

"Perhaps one day we'll have female detectives at Scotland Yard," the inspector chuckled, as though the very idea were so absurd it was amusing.

Mrs. Jeffries shot him a disapproving glance, but he didn't see it. She rather thought women as detectives was an excellent idea. And women doctors, solicitors, bankers, and barristers, too. In short, the world would probably be a much better place if women had equal say in how the world was run. But right now was not the time to have a debate about a woman's place in society. "Did the maid tell you anything else?" she asked Betsy.

"Not much, just that he's a good employer, treats the servants decently, and doesn't work them like dogs." Betsy told them about the rest of her encounter with Justin Vincent's housemaid. She took care to give them all the details, no matter how unimportant they seemed. As Mrs. Jeffries always said, sometimes it was the details that gave you the last little bit needed to solve the case. But as soon as she'd finished, an awkward silence fell. The staff simply wasn't used to discussing their murders with Inspector Witherspoon and Constable Barnes.

The quiet was finally broken by Smythe, who said, "Well, I 'ad a bit of luck today. I tracked down one of Whitelaw's clerks at a pub on Morgan Street." He didn't add that he'd tracked the poor man and crossed his palm with silver to get his information. "Accordin' to 'im, now that the other two partners is dead, Whitelaw gets complete control of the business. Too bad Whitelaw doesn't have any real money, because if he did, he could not only control the firm, he could own it, too."

"He'll have real money soon," Mrs. Goodge interrupted. "Come June, he'll be marrying Fiona Rawlings-Rand."

"Rich is she?" The coachman looked amused.

"As sin. And once she's married to Whitelaw, that'll give him enough money to buy anything he wants."

"I say, Mrs. Goodge," Witherspoon stared at his cook in amazement. Like the rest of the household, he was aware that the cook rarely left her kitchen. "How did you come across that bit of information?"

Mrs. Goodge shrugged modestly. "Oh, it's nothin', really. Just a bit of gossip I picked up." She didn't add that she'd sent word to her cousin's husband's sister who worked in the house down the road from Fiona Rawlings-Rand. There were simply some things she didn't share with anyone.

"So Whitelaw stands to benefit the most from the death of his partners," Constable Barnes mused. "Not only will he have control of the company, but now he's got the money to buy it as well. And being stuck in traffic isn't much of an alibi, if you ask me."

"But Whitelaw has been friends with the victims since they was in school," Mrs. Goodge protested. Despite her firsthand exposure to the realities of murder, there was still a sentimental streak in her makeup. "I can't believe he'd kill his lifelong friends."

"And why wait till now?" Wiggins added.

"Do you know when he got engaged?" Mrs. Jeffries asked the cook. Unlike Mrs. Goodge, she wasn't in the least sentimental. She'd seen plenty of cases where friends who had known one another all their lives suddenly decided the world would be a better place if one of them weren't in it any longer.

"He got engaged at a party over Christmas," Mrs. Goodge continued eagerly. "But he and Fiona Rawlings-Rand have had an understanding for over a year. They had to wait to announce their engagement until the mourning period for her mother had passed. The poor woman died of consumption year before last."

"So Whitelaw couldn't count on havin' any cash until just a few months ago," Smythe muttered. "Women 'ave been known to change their minds before they get that ring on their fingers."

Betsy snorted delicately. "Men change their minds too, you know."

"I know that, Betsy," Smythe said patiently. "I wasn't castin' stones at females. I was just statin' a fact."

Mrs. Jeffries interrupted. "What are you thinking, Smythe?"

He shrugged his powerful shoulders. "Give Whitelaw a month or so to make 'is plans and a month or so to get his disguise. Seems to me the timing's just right."

Smythe tried not to watch Betsy too closely as they took their seats around the kitchen table. Since he'd come in this evenin', he knew he'd been watchin' her like a fox stalking a nice, plump, chicken, but he couldn't help it. Blimpey's information had stunned him.

"Have I got a spot on my face?" Betsy demanded irritably. "You've been starin' at me since you come in this evening."

He grinned sheepishly. "Sorry, didn't mean to. I've got a lot on my mind, that's all."

"Thank goodness that's over," Mrs. Goodge sighed with relish and heaved her ample bulk into her favorite chair. "Right nerve-wrackin', havin' to talk in front of the inspector and Constable Barnes."

"Gives me butterflies in my stomach," Betsy agreed. "Not that the inspector weren't nice about it, but I was scared to death every time one of us opened our mouth."

"Do you think we gave too much away?" Wiggins asked. "I mean, do you think he's goin' to guess this isn't our first investigation?"

That was the question on everyone's mind.

Mrs. Jeffries shrugged slightly. "I don't know. I hope not. But whether we've given the game away or not doesn't matter. We had no choice in the matter."

From the back door they heard a sharp knock and then, a moment later, Luty's voice. "Come on, Hatchet, we ain't got all night. It's gittin' late and I've got to pump that danged banker tomorrow morning."

"Good, Luty and Hatchet are here." Mrs. Goodge poured two cups of tea to have ready.

"Evenin', everyone," Luty cried as she came into the room. She was dressed in a bright red satin dress festooned with ruffles, lace, and sequins. Bright red and black feathers decorated her hat, and she carried a black fur muff tucked under her arm. "Hatchet and I just got back from havin' supper at Lord Amsley's and he knows everything that goes on in the City! I'm burstin' to tell you what I've learned."

"Sit down and have some tea," Mrs. Jeffries smiled. She was glad that neither Luty nor Hatchet had taken offense at being excluded from the meeting with Barnes and Witherspoon, but it had been necessary. It was one thing for Witherspoon to think his staff was devoted enough to try and help him, but Luty and Hatchet were another matter indeed.

"Good evening, everyone," Hatchet said formally as he took his seat. He removed his elegant top hat and placed it carefully on the chair beside him. "I hope everything is in good order."

"We didn't give the game away, if that's what you're worried about," Smythe said. "Leastways, I don't think we did."

Mrs. Goodge poured the tea.

As soon as Luty and Hatchet had a cup in front of them, Mrs. Jeffries said, "Do tell us all your news."

"I don't know if Hatchet has any news," said Luty as she shot her butler a disgusted frown. "He's bein' as tight-lipped as a lawyer at a wake. But I found out plenty." She tossed her muff onto the table.

Everyone jumped back.

"Don't worry," Luty laughed. "It ain't in there. Hatchet made me leave my peacemaker at home tonight."

As Luty's muff generally had in it a loaded Colt .45, the staff had good reason to be cautious when she started tossing it about the room.

"I didn't think it appropriate to take firearms to supper with a distinguished man like Lord Amsley," Hatchet explained. "It simply isn't done. Furthermore, I don't know why Madam persists in carrying that weapon. Perhaps you'll be good enough to help me prevail upon her to lock the wretched thing in a cupboard. London is hardly the Wild West."

"No, it's a lot more dangerous," Luty shot back. She waved her hand impatiently. "Anyways, we ain't got time for this. These folks is waiting to hear what I've found out. You'll never guess who don't have an alibi for the time of either murder." She paused and waited. "Damon Hilliard. We had us a nice little chat with the night porter at his building. Seems Mr. Hilliard told the police he was at his office working on both nights, but the porter told us he'd seen the man sneakin' out the back door.''

"The porter also said that Mr. Hilliard often did that," Hatchet put in. "So I'm not certain we ought to put much store by the information.''

"Where does Hilliard go?" Betsy asked. "I mean, why sneak about like that?''

Hatchet shrugged. "I don't know, but I have some sources working on the problem.''

"You mean you bribed a street lad to follow Hilliard," Luty corrected. "But that's okay, I've crossed a few palms with silver myself to get information I wanted.''

"I rarely need to resort to bribery, as you call it," Hatchet sniffed. "Generally, my subtle but clever questioning elicits all the information I need.''

Luty snorted.

Ignoring her, Hatchet continued, "Today, for instance. By cleverly questioning some of my sources in the City, I learned a great deal about the firm of Hornsley, Frampton, and Whitelaw.''

Mrs. Jeffries nodded in approval. Now they might be getting somewhere. "Go on," she urged.

"Well," he learned forward eagerly. "It seems the firm is one of the most successful privately held companies in the City. In the words of my informant, it's a veritable money-maker and has been for years.''

"If they were makin' so much money," Smythe asked, "why did they let Vincent buy in?''

Hatchet smiled. "They wanted to expand. The plan was to open branch offices in Birmingham and Manchester. Even though the company made plenty of money, that kind of growth is expensive. By letting Vincent in, they acquired the capital they needed without depleting their own cash reserves. Vincent approached them right after Christmas. He'd made investments in a number of other businesses and was looking for more. Hornsley, Frampton, and Whitelaw must have seemed like an excellent opportunity.''

''So Vincent approached them?'' Mrs. Jeffries queried.

''Actually,'' Hatchet hesitated, ''my source wasn't sure on that point, so I don't know.''

''Well, I do,'' Luty said. ''That's what I found out from Lord Amsley. It weren't Vincent that approached the company. It was Hornsley that come to Vincent. Vincent was actually thinking of buying into Hilliard's firm. Hornsley, who it appears bribed one of Hilliard's clerks into feeding him information, found out about Vincent and cornered him one night a while back at his club.''

''But why did he invest 'is money there if 'e was fixin' to go with this Hilliard fellow?'' Wiggins asked.

''Probably because he got a look at both their books,'' Luty replied. ''Like Hatchet said, Hornsley, Frampton, and Whitelaw was pretty successful. From what Elliot told me . . .''

''Elliot?'' Mrs. Goodge interrupted. ''Who's he?''

''She means Lord Amsley,'' Hatchet explained.

''Quit interruptin','' Luty demanded, ''or I'll never get this story told. Like I was sayin', Vincent got a look at both companies' books. One firm's loaded with enough money to buy half the Queen's diamonds and the other's just hangin' on. Which would you invest in?''

''Yes, I see,'' Mrs. Jeffries said. ''So, of course, Hilliard has even more reason to hate Hornsley. He deprived him of an investor.''

Luty nodded. ''Looks like it. Hilliard's got no alibi and lots of reason. Seems to me we should keep an eye on him.''

''We will,'' Mrs. Jeffries agreed. She filed all the information in the back of her mind. It was one more piece of the puzzle, but experience had taught her that trying to put the pieces together too early was pointless. ''It's getting late, though, so we'd better tell you what we learned today.''

For the next half hour they told Luty and Hatchet every little detail, including the information Barnes had shared with them about the police end of the investigation.

''So what do we do now?'' Luty asked. ''Seems to me we don't know which rock to look under this time. Could be the killer is someone connected with the victims' personal lives or it could have something to do with the firm itself. That's a lot of territory to cover.''

''Oh, I forgot to tell you,'' Betsy interrupted.

''Forgot what?'' Mrs. Jeffries asked.

''Madeline Wynn. I found out something about her yesterday. She had a right screamin' match with Peter Hornsley on the afternoon he died. Her maid told me Hornsley came to her house and upset her something fierce.''

''What'd 'e do?'' Wiggins asked curiously.

''The maid didn't know. They had the door closed while they was talkin', but all of a sudden she heard Madeline screamin' at Hornsley to get out. Said if he didn't leave them alone, she'd kill him.''

Mrs. Goodge frowned at the maid. "How could you forget to tell us something that important?"

Betsy felt her cheeks turning red. Everyone was staring at her. She could see the same question in all their eyes. She could hardly admit that she'd been so upset by seeing Raymond Skegit again that she hadn't been able to remember her own name, let alone properly pay attention to her detecting. "I, uh . . ."

"Don't be so 'ard on the lass," Smythe interrupted. "You can't fault her for not sayin' anything. She were probably a bit rattled after she come across me havin' a bit of a dust-up with a bloke on Bernabe Street." He broke off and grinned. "It's me you ought to be yellin' at. I took exception to the way a fellow was beatin' 'is poor 'orse. Betsy came 'round the corner just as things was gettin' really nasty."

"You got in a fight?" Wiggins exclaimed.

"Not really, but I would 'ave if Betsy 'adn't been there to stop me." He gave her a quick glance. "She stopped me from whalin' the tar out of the bloke. Never could abide a man who mistreated 'orses."

Mrs. Jeffries gazed at the two of them curiously. She suspected they were both lying. Betsy was staring at her lap and Smythe's voice, for all its bravado, sounded as hollow as a tin drum.

But why? What had really happened yesterday afternoon?

"Well, there's no harm done then," she said calmly. "I'm glad Betsy was able to prevent you from harming someone, even a horsebeater. You're right, of course, it's quite understandable that Betsy would be upset by such an

incident. We'd all be upset if you were injured while indulging in fisticuffs.''

Betsy finally looked up. She smiled gratefully at the
coachman and then turned to Mrs. Jeffries. "Should I keep
on doggin' Madeline Wynn? I mean, after everything we've
learned today, do you think it's worth pursuing?''

"Everything is worth pursuing," Mrs. Jeffries said
firmly. "Despite the fact that the evidence seems to be
pointing toward the business as being the motive for these
murders, we don't really know what the truth is yet. We
mustn't let ourselves be sidetracked.''

"What do you suggest we do now?" Hatchet asked.

"I think Betsy ought to continue investigating Miss
Wynn," she said, turning to the maid. "Find out if she's
had any unusual meetings in the last month.''

Puzzled, Betsy frowned. "What do you mean?''

"I mean, has Madeline Wynn had any dealings with ruf-
fians or unsavory persons in the last month.''

"You think she might 'ave 'ired someone to kill Hornsley?" Smythe said.

"I think it's possible.''

"But why would she want to kill Frampton, then?" Wiggins asked. "I could see she and Hornsley didn't get
on . . .''

"We don't know that she killed anyone," Mrs. Goodge
interrupted. "Mrs. Jeffries is just sayin' we ought to investigate every possibility, that's all." She looked at the housekeeper. "You want me to keep diggin'?''

"If you wouldn't mind," Mrs. Jeffries replied. "We
really must have more information. Smythe, would you
keep on with Grady Whitelaw? We mustn't lose sight of

the fact that, so far, Whitelaw stands to gain the most from the death of his partners.''

''What do you want us to do?'' Luty asked, gesturing at herself and her butler.

''Unless you've a better idea,'' Mrs. Jeffries said slowly, ''I think you ought to concentrate on Stuart Frampton's alibi and on Damon Hilliard.''

''What about Nyles Hornsley?'' Hatchet asked. ''Shouldn't I try and verify his alibi?''

''If you would, please.'' She made a face. ''I don't like giving Inspector Nivens credit, but his idea of a conspiracy between Frampton and Hornsley to rid themselves of unwanted relatives isn't as farfetched as one would think.''

''The thought of Nivens bein' right sticks in my craw,'' Smythe muttered.

''I expect we'd best get goin,' then,'' Luty said. She stood up as did Hatchet. ''We'll pop in tomorrow evenin' with a full report.''

As soon as they'd left, Betsy started to help Mrs. Goodge clear the tea things off the table.

''I'll take care of the clearin' up,'' Mrs. Jeffries said firmly.

''Are you sure?'' Mrs. Goodge asked.

''Positive. I'm not the least tired. My mind is so active I don't think I could sleep yet.''

''All right. Good night, then,'' said Mrs. Goodge, nodding gratefully, and she shuffled off toward the back stairs.

''I'll just lock up,'' Betsy murmured.

''No, I can do that,'' Mrs. Jeffries smiled kindly. ''You go on up to bed. You look exhausted, Betsy. Go get some rest.''

The girl smiled. "Thank you, Mrs. Jeffries. I am tired."

Betsy found Smythe waiting for her on the first floor landing. He was leaning against the staircase, with his arms crossed over his chest.

Suddenly shy, she looked everywhere but at him.

"Betsy," he said softly, "I'd like to talk to ya."

"I'm tired, Smythe." She couldn't face talking to him tonight. "But thanks for what you did for me. Lettin' on that it was your fault I forgot to tell them about Madeline Wynn. That was right decent of you."

He didn't say anything for a moment. Finally, he said, "It's all right, Betsy. I didn't mind. We're friends. There ain't nothin' I wouldn't do for you."

CHAPTER 8

Mrs. Jeffries gathered the teapot and the cups onto the tray. She carried them over to the sink and laid them on the drain board. They could wait until tomorrow; tonight she didn't want to be distracted by washing them up. She went back to her chair, sat down, and rested her chin in her hands.

This case wasn't going at all well. Even with Constable Barnes feeding them information about the official investigation, she still felt as though they were muddling through in the dark. Like the good constable, she had no faith that Inspector Nivens would catch the real killer.

Think, Hepzibah, she told herself, think. There are bound to be some answers somewhere. But where? What did the notes pinned to the victims mean? Were they nonsense words that had meaning only to the killer? Or were they a genuine clue? What about the weapon? A school house tie. Did that have any significance? She frowned, suddenly annoyed with herself. Of course, it was so obvious. Why hadn't she suggested it to Constable Barnes? Someone really should find out which school the victims had attended. Then she frowned again, annoyed at herself for grasping at straws. The school the victims had gone to didn't matter. Hornsley and Frampton were middle-aged men; if their killer was someone from their schooldays, he would hardly have waited thirty years to kill his victims. She sighed. Dr. Bosworth was probably right. The murderer used an old school tie because it was the sort of object that was easily overlooked. Once gone from the old box it was kept in, or the bottom of a broom cupboard, no one even noticed when it was gone.

"Hepzibah." A soft voice whispered her name.

Mrs. Jeffries jumped and whirled around to see Lady Cannonberry standing in the doorway. "Gracious, you gave me a start."

"I'm sorry, I didn't mean to frighten you," Ruth apologized. "I knocked, you see, and then the back door was unlocked, so I thought I'd pop in and see if you were still up. May I come in?"

Mrs. Jeffries summoned a weak smile. She really would have liked to have continued her solitary thinking, but she didn't want to hurt Ruth's feelings. "Of course you can, but I'm afraid I'm the only one still up."

"That's all right," Ruth said, hurrying over to the table and slipping into a chair next to the housekeeper. "I can't stay long. But I did want to give you my report."

"Report? Oh, yes, yes, of course, your report. Please, go right ahead." Mrs. Jeffries was suddenly so tired she almost yawned. And she was irritated, too. If Lady Cannonberry hadn't interrupted her, she was certain she could have put her finger on what it was about this case that she was missing. Still, one couldn't be rude.

"You'll be very pleased with me," Ruth smiled happily. "I've found out quite a bit. Now, don't worry, I was most discreet."

"I'm sure you were."

"But I must say, I'm appalled, Hepzibah, absolutely appalled that some monster is using Gerald's good name to commit these terrible crimes."

"Yes, we feel the same way," Mrs. Jeffries murmured. She hoped Ruth would be brief and to the point.

"Poor Gerald must be at his wit's end," she said, clucking her tongue sympathetically.

Mrs. Jeffries knew she was in for it. Ruth was not going to be brief. She wondered if she dare ask her to leave and come back tomorrow.

"But as I said," Ruth continued without drawing a breath, "I've found out quite a bit. I've been dying to pop over and tell you, but some of my late husband's relatives came by for a visit and I've been entertaining them. Goodness, that can be such a trial. It's not as if they liked me all that much in the first place. I rather get the feeling that my sister-in-law resents the fact that I'm not in mourning anymore. Well, really, it has been three years. How long is one expected to wear black?"

"How very tiresome for you," Mrs. Jeffries muttered. She was barely listening.

"It hasn't been too terribly awful," Ruth shrugged. "As relatives go, they're not too bad. But they do eat up one's time. This is the first chance I've had to slip out and see you." She laughed. "Now, I suppose I ought to get on with my report. Otherwise, we'll be here all night."

Mrs. Jeffries forced another weak smile. She was suddenly dead tired. But it was a good kind of exhaustion, the kind that let her mind wander aimlessly and, in that state, make all sorts of interesting connections. Why was the killer masquerading as Witherspoon? Was he really out to get the inspector arrested for murder? Could it be a vengeful relative from one of their past cases? Or was the answer so much simpler? Could it be, as Smythe suggested, only a way of gaining access to the victims? Or was there another, more complex reason they hadn't even thought of yet?

"A lot of people don't like Marisole Pulman," Ruth chattered, "but I've always been rather fond of her. She knows ever so much about people, too. She knew all about Peter Hornsley."

Peter Hornsley. The name penetrated Mrs. Jeffries's thoughts. She shook herself slightly; she really must listen to what her guest was saying.

"He was a notorious womanizer," Ruth said earnestly. "It's a wonder his poor wife didn't have a nervous fit the way the man carried on."

Mrs. Jeffries sighed inwardly. This was the same old territory. Ruth hadn't discovered anything new. Perhaps it wouldn't be so terribly awful if she didn't listen all that carefully. "How dreadful," she murmured.

"Mind you," Ruth said, "I don't think womanizing is any reason to be murdered. If that were the case, half the married men in London would be in their graves."

"Yes, I expect so," Mrs. Jeffries agreed. Had Stuart

Frampton and Nyles Hornsley entered into a conspiracy to rid themselves of unwanted relatives? No, she didn't believe that. In the first place, conspiracies had a way of coming apart, and in the second, why go through such an elaborate charade of pretending to be a Scotland Yard detective? However, she wasn't going to ignore anything.

"And George Frampton was quite stingy," Ruth continued. "His second wife is always complaining about the paltry allowance he gives her, but just between you and me and the lamppost, Rosalind Frampton probably married George for his money. Not that she gets much. According to what I heard, all she's going to end up with is the house and a yearly allowance. Still, it'll probably be more than what she had before. I mean, financially she'll be better off with her husband dead than alive. Oh dear, that sounded quite crass. I didn't mean it the way it came out . . ."

"Don't worry, Ruth," Mrs. Jeffries said. "I know what you meant. What else have you found out?"

"Well, Grady Whitelaw, the third partner, is coming into packets of money after he marries Fiona Rawlings-Rand," said Ruth, shaking her head. "I don't see why she wants to marry him. He's ages older than she and not precisely what I would call a 'good catch.' But then again, perhaps she really loves him."

Mrs. Jeffries almost groaned. She completely stopped listening. Ruth hadn't learned anything they didn't already know.

"Of course all three of the men went to school together," Ruth continued eagerly, totally oblivious to the fact that her audience had completely tuned her out. "Marisole knew all about that too. Her husband was at the same school.''

Mrs. Jeffries made a mental note to drop a few hints to Constable Barnes tomorrow. She was more and more convinced these murders had happened because of the business. After all, they'd found out that Damon Hilliard's alibi was worthless. Surely Hilliard wasn't the only one who hated the firm of Hornsley, Frampton, and Whitelaw. And what about Whitelaw? It seemed to Mrs. Jeffries that the man stood to gain an inordinate amount of money and power with the deaths of his partners. Once he married, he could not only finance any expansion, he could probably afford to buy the late partner's shares from their estates.

''It was one of those awful public schools the British are so proud of,'' Ruth sneered. ''Mind you, they did have to hush up that awful scandal about that boy's hand getting so badly burned. Poor child, Marisole's husband said it ruined the lad's life. The other boys lied, you see, so the Osbornes had to take their son out of school.''

Mrs. Jeffries nodded vaguely. Sometimes she forgot that Lady Cannonberry, for all her aristocratic trappings, was really quite a radical. Not that she faulted her for her political opinions, of course. She was in sympathy with many of them herself. ''Scandal,'' she repeated vaguely.

''Oh, it was years ago,'' Ruth waved a hand dismissively. ''And the family left the country after it happened. I believe Marisole said they went to Australia or Canada or . . .'' she hesitated, trying to remember. ''Some such place like that. Anyway, it doesn't matter now. But I did find out there's some sort of scandal attached to Rosalind Frampton. Should I follow that line of inquiry?''

Mrs. Jeffries suspected she knew precisely what the scandal was, too. And they already knew all about it. Constable Barnes had told them. Rosalind Frampton had been an actress before her marriage. Hardly earthshaking, but right now, Mrs. Jeffries would agree to anything to have a bit of peace and quiet.

"That's a wonderful idea," she said.

"Oh good," Ruth beamed with pleasure. "I do so want to help Gerald. I'm so looking forward to going to Edwina Carrington's April ball with him. I want to make sure he enjoys himself. He's such a very good man. He deserves some pleasure in life."

Her statement made Mrs. Jeffries feel small enough to crawl in a tea tin. She ought to be ashamed of herself. She had no right to patronize Ruth. Lady Cannonberry was just as concerned about Inspector Witherspoon as they were and she was doing her best to help.

"Well." Ruth suddenly stood up. "I believe that's about it, then. Tomorrow I'll get out and about and see what I can learn about Rosalind Frampton. Perhaps I'll pop round tomorrow evening, if that's all right."

"Uh, that'll be fine." Mrs. Jeffries got up as well. "Do come round as soon as you hear anything." Guilt-stricken because she hadn't really heard a word that Ruth had said, she tried to make amends. "And do see what else you can learn. Remember, anything you pick up, no matter how insignificant it seems, could be the clue that solves the case."

Ruth smiled happily, delighted to be of service. "Oh yes, I'll remember and I'll keep my ears open. My husband's relatives are leaving tomorrow. I'll have plenty of time to 'go on the hunt,' as they say.''

"I say, Mrs. Jeffries, these eggs are excellent this morning. Mrs. Goodge has really outdone herself." The inspector shoved the last bite of coddled eggs into his mouth and picked up his napkin.

Mrs. Jeffries, who was serving breakfast this morning because Betsy and the others had already gone out, pushed the toast rack closer to his plate. "Yes, she has, sir. Do have more toast. Mrs. Goodge's bread is particularly good today, too."

"Thank you, I believe I will." He reached for what was his third piece. He cleared his throat. He had something important to tell his housekeeper, something he'd thought about for hours last night. He wanted to say it just right. "I must say," he began, "I'm quite amazed by all of you."

"Amazed, sir?" Mrs. Jeffries said cautiously.

He smeared butter and marmalade on the toasted bread. "I don't suppose 'amazed' is really the right word. I should have said I'm touched by how devoted the staff is to me. Gracious, to think they're actually out there in the City, trying to help me clear my name! It's so very kind of all of you." Drat, he thought, why had his speech sounded so much better in his head than it did when he said it aloud.

"We're not being kind, sir." Mrs. Jeffries relaxed. "We're doing for you only what we are sure you would do for us. You are, after all, both an exceptional employer and an exceptional policeman."

Witherspoon smiled proudly. "Well, er, I'm glad you

think so. But there is one thing I must say . . .'' He paused and nibbled on his toast.

Mrs. Jeffries waited patiently. She was relieved he wasn't going to go on about how good the staff was at snooping. That was hitting a bit too close to home. She wasn't sure how much longer she could convince him and Barnes that the information the staff picked up was just luck and not experience. "And what's that, sir?'' she prompted.

He swallowed and took a deep breath. "Whatever happens, I want the staff to know that I'm proud of them and that I know they've done their best.''

She stared at him, not sure she understood exactly what he was trying to tell her.

"But sometimes, despite our best efforts,'' he continued, "the wrong thing happens and justice is not served. But whatever happens, I'll never forget how my household rallied round me and tried to help.''

As she listened to him, that sense of foreboding she'd been plagued with since the start of the case came back to her with a vengeance. Her stomach clenched and a shiver crawled up her spine. She didn't like the tone he used. She didn't like it at all. It was almost as if he was resigned to the worst.

"I assure you, sir, the staff has the utmost confidence in you. The only thing that's going to happen is that we're going to find the real perpetrator of these awful crimes.''

He stared at her for a long moment. "Do you really think so?''

There was a note of desperation in his voice. A note that told Mrs. Jeffries quite clearly that he was dreadfully worried. "Of course I think so, sir. But it would be most helpful if you could remember exactly where you walked on the nights of the murders," she pleaded. "Surely someone must have seen you."

Witherspoon threw his hands up. "But that's just it, I've told Nivens where I was." He looked away, his gaze darting about the dining room as though he'd never seen it before. "But you know, I don't think the chap believes me. As for someone seeing me, well, there's a good explanation for why no one did. Both evenings were wretched. There weren't many people out and about in the wet and the fog."

Mrs. Jeffries knew he was lying, and for the life of her she couldn't understand why. But she knew he wasn't a murderer.

"I'm sure Nivens understands that, sir."

"I don't think so, Mrs. Jeffries," he said, shaking his head. "I have an awful feeling about this case. I'm not ashamed to admit I'm worried. Very worried, indeed."

"That's nonsense, sir," she said bluntly. "You've done nothing wrong. In the end, we'll find the real killer. Now, sir, give me your professional opinion. Why do you think these crimes are being committed?"

He appeared surprised by her sudden change of subject; then he thought about it for a moment and relaxed against the back of his chair. "Well, I've come to the conclusion it has something to do with the firm."

"Yes, I think so too."

"Two partners isn't a coincidence," he continued. "It's the only real connection between the victims. Therefore, I've come to the conclusion it's the firm itself which is under attack."

"But the victims have known each other since their

schooldays,'' Mrs. Jeffries ventured. She agreed with the inspector, but she didn't want to leave any avenue of inquiry unexplored. ''Surely there could be a connection from the past we don't know about.''

He waved his hand in the air dismissively. ''I don't think so. Among the upper classes in Britain, half of London went to school together. So I don't think we can look for any motives from the past. Besides, the victims may have known each other for years, but I haven't seen any evidence that they were genuinely fond of one another. According to what Barnes said, there was a conspicuous absence of grief about the company when Hornsley died. Goodness, they didn't even shut the place for the man's funeral.''

''Whitelaw isn't going to close it for Frampton's funeral either,'' she murmured. She'd picked up that little tidbit from Barnes last night.

''Ah, yes, Whitelaw,'' Witherspoon mused. ''He does quite well out of his partners' deaths, doesn't he?''

''So it would seem, sir.'' She was glad the inspector agreed with her assessment of the situation. The murders probably were centered on the company. All the evidence seemed to point that way. But what if they were wrong? What if it were a conspiracy? What if the killings had nothing to do with the people murdered but were actually just arbitrary, and the murderer's true purpose was to ruin Gerald Witherspoon? The thought depressed her. ''Perhaps we ought to keep a close eye on Mr. Whitelaw.''

''Yes, I certainly hope Barnes is able to do so without Nivens's interference. I should never forgive myself if that man was murdered as well.''

''But he may be the killer, sir.''

"And he might not be," Witherspoon replied.

Mrs. Jeffries said nothing. She was suddenly terribly unsure of herself. She'd no idea what to do next, where to look for answers, or even what to look for!

Witherspoon reached for the last piece of toast. "Appearances aren't always as they seem, Mrs. Jeffries. Whitelaw may be our most likely suspect, but then again, I don't believe that anyone is guilty until I've found evidence proving beyond a shadow of a doubt that they are."

They discussed the case for another half hour; then the inspector decided to he'd take Fred and go for a walk.

Mrs. Jeffries gathered up the breakfast things on a tray and took them down to the kitchen. Wiggins, his face creased in intense concentration, was sitting at the far end of the breakfast table. There was an open notebook in front of him and he had a pencil in his hand.

Mrs. Goodge was bustling about like a general readying troops for battle. A tray of buns was on the counter, a plate of biscuits next to them, and the kettle was whistling furiously.

"Morning, Mrs. Jeffries," the cook said cheerfully, as she flipped a clean linen over the still warm buns. "Did the inspector enjoy his breakfast?"

"He did indeed," Mrs. Jeffries replied. She put the tray of dishes on the drainboard. "What are you doing, Wiggins?"

"Writin'," he replied. "I thought I'd try me hand at writin' a novel. Seems to me it's dead easy. All you got to do is make up some tragic tale and put in lots of bits to make people cry their eyes out."

"I think there is more to it than that," Mrs. Jeffries said carefully. She never liked to discourage people.

"Corse there is," Wiggins agreed, "but it's not like I've got anything else to do right now. Mudies don't open till half past nine. Besides, all it takes to write a book is practice."

She started to point out that it probably took more than just practice, but as he was already depressed about having a sprained ankle and doing nothing but going to lending libraries, she decided to say nothing. Besides, one never knew. Wiggins might be a literary genius. "I think writing a novel is a wonderful idea. You scribble away now, and then when we've time, after this case is over, you can read us what you've written."

From behind her she heard Mrs. Goodge snort. But when she turned to look at the cook, she saw nothing but bland innocence on her broad face.

Mrs. Goodge caught her eye. "Mrs. Jeffries," she asked, "would you help me write a letter this afternoon?"

"Certainly," Mrs. Jeffries replied.

"I can 'elp you," Wiggins volunteered.

"No, no," Mrs. Goodge said quickly. "Thanks all the same, Wiggins, but this is a special letter. It's for a lord." She smiled at the housekeeper. "I've decided not to accept Lord Gurney's offer of a position."

"I'm so glad, Mrs. Goodge," Mrs. Jeffries said earnestly. She smiled. "I was so afraid you were going to leave us, and, frankly, it wouldn't be the same here without you."

Pleased, Mrs. Goodge's cheeks turned a bright pink. Behind her spectacles, her eyes misted. "Well, that's what I thought, too. Lord Gurney is in the past. This is my future.

Truth is, Mrs. Jeffries, after gettin' used to the way we do things here, I don't think I'd much care to go back to a 'proper' household. Besides, Lord Gurney isn't a police detective. There'd be no murders at his house.''

Barnes wasn't sure if he was irritated or amused. Inspector Nivens was actin' like a lovesick cow. He watched Nivens's mouth gape as the lovely young woman came further into the drawing room.

She was tall, dark-haired, and slender with the most perfect complexion Barnes had ever seen. Her nose was small and straight, her eyes a deep blue, and her mouth was full and beautifully shaped. Cor, she was a looker all right, but that didn't excuse Nivens from actin' like a fool.

"I'm sorry to keep you waiting," Madeline Wynn said coolly, "but I wasn't ready to receive visitors."

"That's quite all right," Nivens said quickly. He took a step toward her and stumbled over a footstool. "Oh dear." He glared at the offending piece of furniture. "How clumsy of me. Now, Miss Wynn, we're sorry to have to intrude upon you, but we've some questions to ask."

"Would you like to sit down?" she inquired politely. She gestured to the worn brown settee by the fireplace. "Would you care for a cup of tea?"

"How very kind of you," Nivens said. "But we mustn't put you to any trouble."

Barnes stifled a sigh. They were at this little house in Notting Hill to question a suspect, not to play silly games. Didn't Nivens realize that? But then again, Barnes thought, Nivens wasn't the brightest chap in the force.

Nivens settled himself on the settee. Madeline Wynn sat

down in a balloon-backed chair opposite him. She stared at the policeman patiently, making no attempt to speak, her hands folded demurely in the lap of her light blue day dress.

Nivens cleared his throat. He was staring at the woman like he'd never seen one before. His voice, when he finally spoke, was a rusty croak disturbing the silent room. "Uh, as you've probably guessed, we're here to ask some questions about the recent murders of Peter Hornsley and George Frampton."

"Yes, I'd assumed as much." Her voice was deep and throaty, and very seductive. "But I've no idea why you think I would know anything about it. I barely knew the victims."

"But aren't you engaged to Nyles Hornsley?"

"Yes."

"So, therefore, I assumed you knew the family quite well," Nivens said hesitantly.

"Your assumption was wrong."

Nivens frowned.

Barnes had to turn his face to hide his grin. The girl had good nerves, he'd give her that. She wasn't going to make this easy on Nivens. Good.

"But surely you've met your fiancée's family?"

"Of course," she smiled. "But I'm sure you're also aware of the fact that they weren't too happy Nyles and I were engaged. Especially his brother."

"Mr. Hornsley objected to your impending marriage?" Nivens said.

"Let's not waste one another's time, Inspector," she replied. "Peter Hornsley did everything he could to end my engagement."

"Why?"

"I should think that would be obvious," she said, gesturing around at the small drawing room, her gaze raking over the worn brown velvet curtains at the windows, the old-fashioned and fading furniture, and the tiny fire in the hearth. "I'm not rich."

"You're not rich?" Nivens repeated. "But surely that's no reason to . . ."

Madeline Wynn interrupted. "Peter didn't think I was quite good enough to marry into his family," she said impatiently. "My family is respectable but quite poor by comparison to his. He wanted Nyles to marry well, to increase the family's wealth and position."

Nivens jumped slightly as the front door slammed. Both policemen whirled around just as the drawing room door burst open and Nyles Hornsley charged into the room.

"What's going on here?" he demanded. "Have you been badgering my fiancée?"

"Nyles," Madeline Wynn said softly.

"Mr. Hornsley," said Nivens at the same time. "I'm glad you're here. Miss Wynn was just telling us that your brother didn't approve of your forthcoming marriage."

Nyles Hornsley hurried over to his fiancée and put his arm protectively around her shoulders. He ignored Nivens's statement. "You've no right to badger her," he said angrily. "She's nothing to do with these murders."

"We're only asking questions, Mr. Hornsley," Nivens snapped.

"It's all right, Nyles," Madeline said. "I don't mind talking with the police. I've nothing to hide."

"In that case, Miss Wynn," Nivens said quickly,

"would you please tell us if you were acquainted with Mr. George Frampton?"

"I'd met the man once or twice," she replied. "So, yes, I was acquainted with him."

"And you, Mr. Hornsley," Nivens asked, "you knew Mr. Frampton as well?"

"Of course I did. He was Peter's partner. Really, Inspector, you're wasting our time. Neither Madeline nor myself had any reason to murder George Frampton. She barely knew the man."

"Are you both acquainted with Mr. Stuart Frampton?" Nivens pressed.

"What a ridiculous question." Nyles frowned. "Of course I know Stuart, so does Madeline. But what's that got to do with anything?"

Nivens smiled slyly. "Well, sir, perhaps you and Miss Wynn didn't have a reason for murdering George Frampton, but his son certainly did."

"Exactly what are you implying?"

"I'm implying nothing," Nivens said. "I'm merely asking a few questions. Tossing a few ideas about, as they say."

"You're being ridiculous," Nyles said with a sneer. "Stuart didn't murder his father."

"Perhaps he didn't, sir," Nivens shrugged. "He has an alibi for the time of that murder."

"That murder?" Madeline repeated.

"But he doesn't have a particularly good one for the time of your brother's murder," Nivens said.

Barnes cleared his throat, trying vainly to get Nivens's attention. The silly git was going to ruin everything if he kept talking.

"And you, Mr. Hornsley, don't have a very good alibi for the time that George Frampton was killed," Nivens continued.

Barnes shuffled his feet and twitched his shoulders. Nivens ignored him.

Hornsley's brows drew together pensively, as though he couldn't understand what Nivens meant. But Madeline understood.

"You're trying to say that Nyles murdered George Frampton and Stuart murdered Peter Hornsley?" She looked amused by the notion.

"I'm not trying to say anything." Nivens stuck his nose in the air. "But I find it interesting that you should jump so quickly to that conclusion."

Madeline laughed. "In other words, Inspector, we're conspirators."

"You said it, Miss Wynn, not I." Nivens looked inordinately pleased with himself.

Barnes was furious. The fool was telling them the only decent working theory they had. The constable didn't think much of it; in his experience, conspiracies had a way of unraveling. But be that as it may, it was right stupid to let the chief suspects know you had them under your eye.

"Oh, this is absurd," Nyles snapped.

"I think the police must be desperate if they're reduced to that sort of a silly idea," she replied, ignoring her fiancé and glaring disdainfully at Nivens.

"Madeline, let me handle this," Nyles cried, giving her shoulders a tiny shake to get her attention. "You've no idea about these sort of things. So, please, don't say anything else." He turned to Nivens. "Inspector, this is the most

ridiculous thing I've ever heard. You've absolutely no evidence of such a conspiracy because my fiancée and I had
nothing to do with murdering anyone.''

"I've made no accusations," said Nivens, lifting his
chin. "As I said a few moments ago, I'm merely tossing a
few ideas about.''

"Kindly take your absurd ideas and leave," Nyles ordered. He jerked his chin toward the door. "We're not
obliged to stand here and take this kind of abuse.''

"Would you both care to come to the station and help
us with our inquiries?'' Nivens asked.

"That will be fine.'' Nyles's eyes narrowed. "Of course,
we will insist that my solicitor be sent for.'' He was calling
the inspector's bluff and they both knew it.

"Actually, I don't think that will be necessary at this
time,'' Nivens said quickly.

Barnes felt like strangling his superior.

"As a matter of fact,'' Nyles continued, "neither of us
will answer any more questions unless we've a solicitor
present.''

"I see.'' Nivens looked perplexed. He shot Barnes a
quick glance. "In that case, I suppose we'd better leave.
But I do warn you, sir''—he turned back to Nyles Hornsley—"this investigation is far from over. If necessary,
we'll ask both you and Miss Wynn to accompany us to the
station for questioning. You may, of course, have your solicitor present then.''

Betsy was depressed. She crossed Ladbroke Grove and
started for the Notting Hill High Street. She might as well
take an omnibus home. So far today she'd learned nothing.

Her feet hurt and she felt like she'd walked halfway round London. So far today she'd been to Whitelaw's, Vincent's, and now Madeline Wynn's. But she might as well have stayed in bed this morning. She hadn't been able to find anyone to talk to except a footman over at the Vincent house.

So she'd come to Notting Hill hoping to learn something from one of Madeline Wynn's servants. But that hadn't gone right either. She'd hung about in front of Madeline Wynn's house until she'd spotted Constable Barnes and Inspector Nivens coming down the road. Knowing servants as she did, she was sure that no one who worked in that house was coming out anytime soon. Not with the excitement of policemen coming and going.

It was a completely wasted morning. The only thing she'd gotten out of the footman from Vincent's house was that he was a nice master and he liked to wear fancy kid gloves all the time. The Whitelaw house had been shut up tighter than a bank on Sunday, and the police were at Madeline Wynn's. Blast. She hoped the others were doing better than she was.

She dodged around a fruit vendor and kept on walking. Truth was, she felt a bit guilty. She knew she wasn't giving this case her best effort. She could have pumped that footman more, but she hadn't. And she could have hung around a bit longer at the Whitelaw place, but she hadn't. Eventually, the servants would have come out of the Wynn house, but she hadn't bothered to wait.

She was too worried. What on earth was she goin' to tell Smythe? Oh, he'd been real good about not asking her nosy questions. He hadn't poked and pried too hard. But she could see the worry in his eyes every time he looked at her.

She rounded the corner and came to a dead stop. Her heart leapt into her throat and her stomach tightened. Raymond Skegit's carriage was pulling up on the other side of the road. She stared at it for a moment, saw the door opening and a dark-haired man emerging.

From this distance, she couldn't tell if it was Skegit or not. But Betsy was taking no chances. She turned and ran back the way she'd just come.

She darted past a row of shops, dodged the fruit vendor's cart, and leapt into a small, dark passage separating two tall, narrow brick buildings.

From behind her, she thought she heard footsteps, but she didn't look back, she just kept on going.

Her feet pounded against the old cracked walkway, her heart kept time with her feet. God, what was she going to do? Raymond Skegit wasn't someone to mess about with. She'd been lucky three years ago. She couldn't count on being lucky twice. Why had she had the horrible misfortune to run into the bastard again? Why couldn't he have stayed in the East End where he belonged?

She flew out of the passageway and into the road. She tried to dodge around a tall, broad-shouldered man blocking her path, but at the last moment he turned.

Betsy came to a sudden halt as a pair of strong arms reached out and grabbed her around the waist. "What's the 'urry, lass?"

She let out a yelp before she realized who had hold of her. When she saw who it was, she hurled herself into his arms. "Thank God, it's you, Smythe."

CHAPTER 9

⟨◦◦◦⟩

"What's wrong, Betsy?" Smythe asked anxiously. "You come barrelin' out of there like the devil 'imself was on yer 'eels."

When Betsy realized she was still clinging to his neck, she pulled away, her face turning red.

For a moment they stared at each other. The worried expression on his face sent a shaft of guilt straight through her. What could she tell him? The truth? But she didn't know if he would understand. Betsy wasn't sure whether she was ready to risk him finding out the worst about her.

"Betsy," he prompted, giving her a light shake.

"I had a bit of a scare, that's all," she replied, glancing quickly over her shoulder to make sure those footsteps she'd heard had only been in her imagination.

Smythe followed her gaze. "Was someone chasin' ya, then?" He pulled away from her and started toward the darkened passageway she'd just come out of. "Maybe they'd like to deal with the likes of me instead of a slip of a girl like you.''

She grabbed his arm. ''No one was following me.''

''Then why were you running like that?''

She hesitated, undecided. In a split instant, she decided to tell him the truth—the whole truth. What was the point in trying to hide it? If Smythe didn't know her by now, he never would. His opinion of her mattered, it mattered more than she'd ever thought possible. But she hadn't done anything wrong. If he didn't understand what she'd done and, more importantly, why she'd done it, he wasn't worth as much to her as she'd hoped.

''I thought I saw Raymond Skegit's carriage,'' she said, watching his face. ''So I nipped down that passageway thinkin' I could get away from him. I'm scared of him, Smythe. Really scared. He's an awful person, not one to forget a wrong done him.''

Smythe nodded slowly, taking care to keep his expression blank. ''And Skegit thinks you wronged him.''

Betsy swallowed the sudden lump in her throat. ''That's right. He . . .''

''Don't tell me yet, Betsy,'' Smythe gestured at the busy street corner just ahead. ''Whatever you've got to say to me can wait until we're alone and we can talk properly.''

''But . . .''

''Now don't get het up, lass.'' He took her by the elbow and started for the corner. ''I'm not sayin' I don't want to 'ear. I do. But I don't want to 'ave to be askin' you to repeat yerself every other word 'cause the traffic's so loud. What you've got to tell me is important, it's to be treated with respect. We'll talk tonight after the others 'ave gone to bed.''

"But . . ."

"Tonight, Betsy," he ordered softly.

"All right," she replied, thinking that maybe he was right. Saying what she had to say was going to be hard enough. She didn't want to have to say it twice. She only hoped her nerve would hold up long enough. "Tonight it is. But where are we goin' now?"

"To get you in a 'ansom."

"A hansom? Have you lost your mind? I can take an omnibus home." She tugged her arm free and came to a dead stop. "I'm not ready to go home yet. It's still early. I haven't found out much today and I want to keep at it."

"Cor blimey, Betsy, you've just had the wind scared out of ya and ya don't want to go 'ome?" Women, he would never understand them. He wanted her back at Upper Edmonton Gardens. He wanted her safe from the likes of Skegit, at least until he took care of the bastard.

"Well, I'm over it," she snapped. "I'll admit I was frightened. But I had sense enough to run. If I keep my eyes open, I can stay out of Skegit's way."

"You should be 'ome," he said stubbornly. Blast a Spaniard, anyway. Why couldn't the lass see he only wanted what was best for her?

She stuck her chin out, a sure sign that she was digging her heels in. "I can't go home, I've found out nothing."

"That doesn't matter."

"It bloomin' well does. I don't want to be sittin' there tonight when all the rest of you are talkin' about everything you've learned and all I've got to report is that Justin Vincent has more gloves than the prince of Wales.''

Smythe struggled to keep a grin off his face. ''That might be a real valuable clue, Betsy.''

''Right.'' Her voice dripped sarcasm. ''Just like the fact that Rosalind Frampton overspends at her dressmaker's and Nyles Hornsley likes to dance is important.'' She gestured furiously with her hands. ''You see, I've found out nothing important. Nothing at all.''

He stared at her thoughtfully, the urge to smile completely gone. Betsy's eyes were haunted, desperate looking. He realized doing her fair share to help solve the inspector's cases was very important to her. Smythe understood that. It was important to him, too. Not just because they all admired Inspector Witherspoon, though that was a big part of it. But because of the way it made them feel inside themselves when they'd done a good job. It made them feel like they were more than just servants, more than just the forgotten people at the bottom of the heap. But he didn't want her roaming around the streets of London, even in the daytime. Not alone. Not until he'd taken care of Raymond Skegit. Bloomin' Ada, he couldn't order her back to Upper Edmonton Gardens.

Suddenly, he saw a solution. ''I've got an idea,'' he said, taking her arm again and starting toward the corner.

''What idea?'' She stared at him suspiciously. ''Where we goin? I've told you, I'm not through for the day.''

''We're goin' up to the corner to grab a 'ansom,'' he replied quickly, as she was trying to jerk her elbow from his grip. ''And I don't want you to go home. I want you to come with me over to the City.''

"Why?" Her tone was still suspicious, but also interested as well.

"Cabbie," he yelled, dropping her arm and waving a hand at a passing hansom. The cab stopped and he pulled the door open. "Get in," he said. "I'll tell you all about it as we go."

"Do you know how much a cab to the City is goin' to cost?" she hissed, giving the driver a worried glance.

Her words reminded him he had a few shameful secrets of his own. He shrugged and looked over her shoulder, unwilling to meet her eyes. "Don't fret over it, lass," he lied, grabbing her elbow and practically shoving her inside. "I 'ad a good day at the racecourse last week, so we can ride in style today."

"You ought to be savin' your money," she mumbled, but she got in the hansom anyway. Smythe climbed in after her.

"All right," Betsy said as soon as they started off, "tell me about this idea of yours."

"I thought we'd pool our resources," he said casually, thinking as he spoke. "Mrs. Jeffries is convinced the murders had something to do with the firm, right?"

"That's what she said this morning."

"So I was thinkin' why don't you and I go over to Hornsley's office and see if we can 'ave a nice little chat with someone on 'is staff."

"You mean the clerks and such?"

"Not just the clerks," he replied, "but maybe they have a tea lady or charwoman or someone like that."

"I don't know, Smythe." She looked doubtful. "It's the

middle of the day. How are we going to get to them? They'll all be working.''

"They've got to have a meal break, don't they?''

Betsy wasn't so sure that was true. "I don't know, do they?''

"I've seen the clerks in the pubs and such when I've been 'round that part of town. So I think we ought to give it a try.''

"What were you doin' over in the City?'' she asked curiously.

He looked out the small, narrow window. "Uh, on the inspector's cases and such. You know, when I'm out and about.'' He could hardly admit that his odious banker was always pesterin' him about his money.

Betsy seemed to accept that. "All right,'' she said, giving him a bright smile, "let's have a go at it, then. We'll see what we can find out.''

Smythe sighed inwardly in relief. Short of tying the girl to his wrist he couldn't think of a way to keep her safe. But at least the City of London was the last place that Skegit was likely to show up. And if Skegit did appear, Smythe wouldn't be far from Betsy at all.

Luty stopped in front of the house and squinted at the brass number plate. Number twelve . . . or was that an eight instead of a two? Dang it, anyway, she hated gettin' old. She hadn't minded when her feet went a bit arthritic, and she didn't mind all the aches and pains her stomach would give her when she ate that hot, spicy food her fancy French chef hated fixin'. But dang it, she hated losin' her eyesight.

When she was a girl, she could spot an eagle on a

tree branch half a mile away. Now she was lucky if she could make out a blasted house number. She started up the stairs. This had better be number twelve or she was goin' to be mighty mad.

She banged the brass door knocker loudly against the painted black door. Even before she'd started tryin' to read them piddly little house numbers, she'd been in a bad mood. Who would have guessed that her friend Myrtle would pick this case to start asking questions about? Dang Myrtle, anyway. Why'd she have to start gettin' curious all of a sudden?

She'd gone to Myrtle's this morning to pump her for some information. But the silly cow had a bad cold and her ears was plugged up. Luty had to repeat everything twice to make herself understood.

And Myrtle was in a bad mood, actin' like a bear with a thorn in its paw. The minute Luty had started askin' questions, Myrtle's little pig eyes had narrowed and she'd asked why Luty only dropped by to ask her questions about people Luty didn't even know? Well, it was danged obvious that Myrtle wasn't goin to be cooperative, not with that cold. So Luty had told her she'd be back when Myrtle wasn't feelin' so poorly, and then she left.

Luty glared at the closed door. What was takin' 'em so long? Irritably, she pounded the knocker again. Course she felt a little bad, since Myrtle was such a lonely soul. That's why she was always gaddin' about so much. And it wouldn't hurt to drop by every now and again just to visit with the woman. Luty promised herself she'd go see Myrtle again as soon as this case was over and she had more free time.

The door flew open and a tall, bald-headed butler, lookin' even stiffer than Hatchet on a bad day, was starin' down his nose at her. "Yes, madam?" he said frostily. "May I help you?"

Luty lifted her chin, raised her sable muff a notch higher and stared him straight in the eye. "I wish to see Mr. Grady Whitelaw."

"Are you an acquaintance of Mr. Whitelaw?"

"I don't reckon that's really any of your business. But I've already been to his office and they told me he'd come home. So, if you don't mind, I'd appreciate you tellin' him I'm here."

"I'm afraid that's not possible." He started to close the door.

Luty wasn't going to be beaten twice in one day. She slammed her hand flat against the door, shoved it as hard as she could and charged past the butler.

"Really, madam . . ." the butler sputtered.

"I'd appreciate it if you'd tell Mr. Whitelaw I'm here," she repeated haughtily. Then she turned her back on him and started down the black-and-white tiled hallway. Most of these fancy houses were all alike; she'd find a place to sit while ol' stiff-neck rustled up Whitelaw. "I'll wait in the drawing room."

"But, madam," the butler yelped. But Luty had made good her escape and was turning in to the double doors leading to the drawing room. He charged after her.

Luty whirled about as she heard the servant's running footsteps. "Are you deaf, man? I said I'd like to speak to Mr. Whitelaw and I ain't goin' to budge from this room till I see him. Now go git him."

"Mr. Whitelaw isn't here," the butler yelled. He was totally frazzled. One simply did not pick up elegantly dressed old ladies and toss them out the front door, no matter how much one was tempted. Besides, this one looked as if she might object to the whole proceedings.

"Well, where in the dickens is he?"

"Paying a mourning visit. A dear friend has just died and he's paying a condolence call on the family." That ought to shame the woman.

"Nell's bells. When's he due back?"

He couldn't believe his ears. This person obviously had no shame. "I really can't say, madam."

"Name's Crookshank. Luty Belle Crookshank. What's yours?"

The question so startled him he answered without thinking. "Payne, madam. Now, I'm afraid I must ask you to . . ."

"Maybe you can help me, Payne," she said. "You see, I left my shawl in a hansom cab night before last. I dropped it on the floor as I was leavin', you see."

"I see . . ." Payne didn't see anything.

"Well, my friend Myrtle told me she happened to see Mr. Whitelaw get in that very hansom right after I got out of it. Now, I've already checked with the driver and he claims there weren't no shawl on the floor when he got back to the depot, so I figure Mr. Whitelaw must have brung it home with him. Can you run upstairs an' git it for me?"

Run upstairs? Payne had never run up the stairs in his life. "Madam, I assure you, Mr. Whitelaw doesn't have your shawl in his possession."

"Now, I ain't accusin' him of stealin' it," Luty said quickly. "And normally I wouldn't make a fuss over a pink lace shawl, but this one was real special. A friend of mine made it for me and she's dead now. So you see, I'd like to have it back. You just go on upstairs and have a peek in Mr. Whitelaw's drawers. I'll bet he was meanin' to try and find the owner."

"I'm sorry, Mrs. . . . er . . ."

"Crookshank."

"Mrs. Crookshank." Payne's head began to pound. "But I believe your friend must have made a mistake . . ."

"Oh no, Myrtle saw Mr. Whitelaw git into that cab. She was waitin' on the door stoop when it dropped me off, and she knows who Mr. Whitelaw is, ya see, and he got in right behind me. The driver says it was his last run of the night, and he ain't got my shawl, so Mr. Whitelaw has to have it."

Payne shook his head. This woman was obviously of unsound mind. Perhaps he ought to be a bit gentler with her. "I'm sorry," he said kindly, "but that's impossible."

"Are you callin' me a liar?" Luty demanded.

"No, madam, but your friend must have made a mistake." His good intentions disappeared.

"Myrtle don't make mistakes like that. Not about my shawl. She knows how important it is to me, so you git yourself up those stairs and see if you can find it."

"I tell you," Payne's voice began to rise, "your shawl isn't here."

"Yes, it is."

They were both shouting now.

"It couldn't be here," Payne yelled.

"How do ya know?" Luty bellowed. "Ya ain't even looked yet."

"I know because Mr. Whitelaw wasn't in a hansom at all. He walked to his destination. He'd forgotten his gloves, you see, and a *gentleman* doesn't call upon his fiancée without gloves, so one of our footmen went after him. But he didn't catch up with him. He lost sight of Mr. Whitelaw at Hyde Park Corner."

Luty smiled in satisfaction. That was precisely what she needed to know.

"Thank you," Constable Barnes said to Betsy. He reached for the cup of tea she'd poured. "I need this. Nivens was even worse today than usual. Drug us all over London and we didn't learn a bloody thing."

They were all gathered round the dining room table. Barnes had popped in for a late tea on his way home.

"I'm sure Inspector Nivens is doing the best he can," Witherspoon said kindly.

"He may be," Barnes shot back irritably. "But he doesn't know how to conduct a proper murder investigation. We learned nothing today. On top of that, Nivens lost his temper when we were questioning Madeline Wynn and Nyles Hornsley. He got so rattled he told them his conspiracy theory. Well, he told 'em enough so that they figured it out."

"Do you believe Inspector Nivens's idea is correct?" Mrs. Jeffries asked.

Barnes sighed. "No. But whether it were a good theory or not, Nivens had no business lettin' on to two of our main suspects that we was thinkin' along those lines. It's not much of an idea, but it's all we've got so far.''

"What about the theory that the murders have something to do with the business and not the victims' personal lives?" Witherspoon asked. "Have you found anything new along those lines?"

Again Barnes sighed. "Not a bloomin' thing. I spent a few hours over in the City today, talking to clerks and bankers and the like, but I didn't find out much. The firm isn't highly thought of by its competitors, but it's not much worse than some of the other insurance firms."

"How about Mr. Hilliard?" Betsy asked timidly. "Is he still a suspect?"

"Near as I can tell, everyone's a suspect. I haven't learned anything about Hilliard that would clear him. We know he was lyin' about bein' in his office on the nights of the murders."

Betsy glanced at Smythe, who nodded his head slightly.

"Constable Barnes," she said. "I think you can scratch Damon Hilliard off your list of suspects."

Barnes's eyebrows shot up. "What have you found out?"

"We were over in the City today, seeing what we could find out. I happened to run into the charlady that does Hilliard's office." Betsy hadn't run into the charlady; she'd tracked the woman down like a bloodhound. But Barnes didn't need to know that. "And she told me something right interesting."

"Go on, Betsy," Witherspoon encouraged. Gracious, he'd never thought that the girl was so devoted to him. Imagine, going all the way over to the City. "Tell us what you've heard."

Betsy blushed slightly. This was goin' to be the hard part. "Mrs. Miller," she began, "that's the charlady, she's quite a chatty kind, you see. She told me that Hilliard slips out of his office two or three times a week. He goes to a . . ." she broke off, searching for the right word.

"He goes to a brothel," Smythe said quietly. He could see that Betsy was having a devil of a time speaking frankly. He wondered if it was because the inspector and Barnes were here. Usually the lass hadn't a bit of trouble speakin' her mind, no matter what the subject. He gave the maid an understanding smile. "Betsy told me about it when we was comin' 'ome tonight."

"Was he at the brothel," Witherspoon felt his own cheeks flaming, "on the nights of the murders?"

Smythe nodded. "Yes. He were there last Friday night when Hornsley was done in and again on Monday night when Frampton got it." He hoped the policemen wouldn't ask him how he'd found out all the details about Hilliard's activities. Not after the row he and Betsy had had about it this afternoon. Blimey, it wasn't like he'd gone into that place for the fun of it! Besides, he'd made sure that Betsy was safely in the hansom while he was inside. Not that she appreciated his gesture. She'd pouted all the way home.

"Well, that lets Hilliard out, then." Barnes took a sip of tea. "But I'll have to confirm his alibi." He smiled apologetically at Smythe. "Not that I'm doubtin' you . . ."

"It's all right," Smythe said quickly. "We understand you can't just take our word for it." He glanced at Betsy. "Go on, tell 'em what else you found out."

"What else?" she repeated in confusion. Then she saw the mischievous twinkle in his eyes. "Oh yes, I found out that Justin Vincent has more gloves than the prince of Wales."

"That's odd," Barnes murmured, "Vincent didn't strike me as a particularly vain man." He wasn't sure exactly what this last piece of information could possibly have to do with the murder, but he didn't want them to feel like he was taking their efforts lightly. The truth was, he was quite impressed by everything they had found out. "But guess you can't really tell much about a person by just lookin' at them. Anyway, did you learn anything else?" he asked the coachman.

"Not much," Smythe shrugged. "Just picked up a bit more gossip about them break-ins the buildin' 'ad the month or so before the first killin'. Seems right strange, but one of the clerks told me the only firm that got broken into was Hornsley, Frampton, and Whitelaw. And the only thing that was done was someone overturned the inkwells onto the desks and broke the pens into bits." He grinned. "He said that Hornsley almost had a conniption fit when he come in and found ink all over his fancy rosewood desk."

"That sounds like a schoolboy prank, not a proper break-in," Mrs. Goodge said derisively.

"I don't think it means anything," Barnes said. "I spoke to the lads that were called there when it happened. According to the report, there wasn't anything stolen. It was more a case of malicious mischief than anything else. But Police Constable Turgen told me that the incident shook the tenants up so badly that they hired that night watchman. Not that it did much good, though. Hornsley was still murdered right under the man's nose. Oh well, perhaps we'll make sense of it yet." He smiled at the others. "But you've done well. Today hasn't been wasted."

"Of course it hasn't, Barnes," Witherspoon said quickly. "All information is useful in some way or other." He beamed at his staff. "I must say, I'm amazed. You've all learned so very much. Why, it's almost as if you've done this before."

"Thank you, sir," Mrs. Jeffries said quickly. She turned to Barnes. "What have you learned today, Constable?"

Barnes told them every little detail about his day with Inspector Nivens. He could barely keep the disgust out of his voice. When he'd finished, he looked around at the circle of disappointed faces. "Not much, is it?"

"A good day's work, sir," Mrs. Goodge said stoutly. Honestly, they ought to make women detectives. They knew how to talk to people. "You've done your best, and that's what counts. I've learned a bit myself today. It's not much, mind you, but like I always say, you never know what's goin' to season the soup until it's done good and proper. So here's my bit. It seems that Grady Whitelaw wasn't at home on the night of Hornsley's murder." She paused, waiting for the effect her words would have on the others. And she wasn't disappointed by their avid attention. "Accordin' to my sources, he wasn't at home alone at all. He was out somewhere's else. I know because my source told me she saw him comin' home last Friday night quite late. She said saw Whitelaw slippin' in through the side entrance to his own house instead of usin' the front door."

Barnes stared at her incredulously. "Would you mind tellin' me who this source is?"

Mrs. Goodge shifted uneasily. Admitting she'd sent one

of the street lads (whom she occasionally fed cakes and buns to) over to snoop about in Whitelaw's neighborhood would never do. She didn't want Barnes or Witherspoon to know about that. Why, they'd figure out in an instant that this wasn't the first time they'd been snoopin' about.

"Well, I found out through a bit of gossip," she hedged. "A friend of mine knows the maid that lives next door to Grady Whitelaw."

"And was it this maid who saw Mr. Whitelaw coming in late on the evening of March ninth?" Witherspoon asked.

"Right," agreed Mrs. Goodge. She looked quickly at Mrs. Jeffries for guidance. The housekeeper nodded almost imperceptibly.

"It was a Friday night, you see," Mrs. Goodge continued, "and her employers was out for the evening. The girl took advantage. She slipped out while they was gone to meet her sweetheart."

"So we could call this girl to give evidence in a trial?" Barnes pressed.

"I suppose so," Mrs. Goodge said slowly. "But I don't think she'd like it much."

"Do you know her name? I'd like to talk with her. This could be important evidence," Barnes said.

Mrs. Goodge thought quickly. "Her name's Margaret Turner. But I don't think you ought to talk to her unless you really have to make an arrest. If her employers found out what she'd done, she'd lose her position."

"Oh dear, we wouldn't want that to happen," Witherspoon agreed. "I say, Barnes, let's not bother the girl unless we find additional evidence that Whitelaw had something to do with the murders. I don't want anyone losing their positions."

Luty and Hatchet arrived as soon as supper was finished. Mrs. Jeffries and the others told them everything they'd heard from Barnes.

"I didn't get to tell the inspector and Constable Barnes what I'd learned today," Wiggins complained as soon as the housekeeper had finished speaking. "And I found out all kinds of things."

"All right, boy," Luty said kindly, "you go ahead and tell us. My news can wait."

"Yes, Wiggins," Mrs. Jeffries added. "It was most unkind of us to ignore you during our meeting with the constable."

Wiggins shifted uncomfortably. He wished he hadn't raised such a fuss. He hadn't learned all that much. "Well," he said slowly, "tomorrow's the Ides of March."

Everyone stared at him. He felt his cheeks burn with embarrassment. "I'm not tellin' this right," he cried. "What I meant to say was that I think them words pinned on the dead men's chest might be Latin."

"Since when do you know Latin?" Mrs. Goodge asked.

"I don't know it," Wiggins said, "but I can read, and today while I was at Mudies I come across this quote. It caught my eye 'cause the letters was just like the ones in the notes." He dug in his pocket and pulled out a piece of string, a sweet covered in lint, and finally a scrap of paper.

" 'Ere it is," he said, smoothing the paper out on the table. "Veni, vidi, vici," he read aloud. "VENI was the word written on Hornsley's paper, VIDI was the one written on Frampton's chest, so I figured it had to mean something.''

"I came, I saw, I conquered," Hatchet translated. "I do believe he's right. Well done, Wiggins. How fortunate for us that you happened across a volume of Suetonius.''

"I came, I saw, I conquered," Luty repeated. "But what's it mean?''

"Obviously, it means something to the killer," Hatchet replied.

"But what that could possibly be is the difficult part,'' Mrs. Jeffries mused. "How on earth can we determine what it means? A quote, even a famous one, taken out of context is virtually meaningless unless one can determine what it means to the killer.''

"You mean this is useless?" Wiggins gestured helplessly at the scrap of paper. "But I spent hours pourin' over them books, and they didn't even have pretty plates or illustrations.''

"Of course it isn't useless," Mrs. Jeffries said quickly. "It's merely a matter of us using our eyes, ears, and brains to determine why the killer would put such a thing on his victims' bodies.'' She knew it wasn't going to be easy. That kind of a quotation could mean just about anything.

"While we're thinkin' about it," Luty said, "can I tell everyone what I found out?'' She paused a moment, waiting for their approval and then plunged straight ahead, telling them about her encounter with Grady Whitelaw's butler. "So I found out exactly what we needed to know. Not only does Whitelaw not have an alibi, but he was seen practically at the scene of the crime only minutes before Frampton was killed.''

"I'd say that just about proves 'e's our killer," Smythe said softly. He glanced at the clock and saw that time was getting on. He hoped this meeting wouldn't last all night. He still had to talk to Betsy, and then he had to go out.

"The evidence certainly does seem to be pointing at Whitelaw," Mrs. Jeffries replied. But something was wrong. That little voice in the back of her mind was telling her that something was definitely wrong about this case. Something so obvious that it was almost a case of not being able to see the forest for the trees.

"So what do we do now?" Luty asked.

"I think we should keep on digging," Mrs. Jeffries said.

"Are we goin' to tell the inspector and Constable Barnes about what they've"—she gestured at Luty, Wiggins and Hatchet—"found out?"

"Yes, but that can wait until tomorrow."

Betsy waited until she heard Mrs. Jeffries's door close and then she crept down the stairs and into the kitchen. The big room was in darkness save for a single candle in the center of the table.

"Come on in, lass," Smythe said softly. "I've been waitin' for ya."

She was grateful for the dim light. It would help her, make it easier for her if she couldn't see his face so clearly.

She took the chair opposite him. "I had to wait till I heard Mrs. Jeffries go up," she explained, wanting to put off the truth as long as possible.

"I know," he grinned. "I 'ad to wait till Wiggins fell asleep. He were snorin' like a drunken lord when I left." He stopped and his smile faded. "All right, lass, tell me about you and Skegit. But before ya say anything, I want ya to know I'll not be sittin' in judgment on ya. I've been poor too and I know we all do things we don't like just so's we can survive."

Betsy blinked to hold back the tears that welled in her eyes. "Thank you," she replied formally. "I appreciate your sayin' that." She took a deep breath. "Raymond Skegit is a . . . a . . ."

"I know what 'e is, Betsy."

She nodded. "Anyways, I was livin' over the East End, me and my mum and my two sisters. Mum worked as a barmaid, and my sisters and I did sewin' and piecework. It weren't much of a livin' but it was enough to keep us in a room to ourselves and buy food and tea. We lived like this for a long time, leastways it seemed like a long time. My older sister got married and left," she swallowed heavily, "and my younger sister died of fever. Mum lost her job at the pub because she'd stayed home and nursed my sister instead of goin' to work. Things seemed to get worse after that. Mum couldn't get work, the clothin' factory that give me the piecework shut down, and we was turned out into the street. We stayed in doss houses for the most part, it weren't too bad, 'cause it was summer. But I'd run into Skegit every now and again, and he'd always ask me to come work for him. He was always at me, tellin' me how much money I could make, how much easier life would be if I worked for him. I wouldn't. No matter how poor we was, I wasn't doin' that." She looked down at the table.

"But then Mum got real sick. By this time it was winter and I was scared to death I was goin' to lose her. So I went to Skegit and told him I'd become one of his girls." She laughed bitterly. "Skegit give me five pounds, told me to use it to get Mum some medicine and a decent place to stay. I thought it was a fortune. I went back to the doss house where I'd left her . . ." Her voice broke. "And she was dead."

"It's all right, lass," Smythe started to get up, but she waved him back to his seat.

"No, let me tell you the rest." She swiped at the tears rolling down her cheeks. "Mum was gone and I was on my own. I used the money Skegit had give me to get her buried. It weren't much, but at least she had a coffin. Then I went to Skegit and told him I wasn't goin' to work for him. He started screamin' at me, callin' me names and tellin' me I owed him five pounds. I give him what little I had, but he didn't want the money. He wanted me." She sighed heavily, as though a great weight had been lifted off her shoulders. "I knew I couldn't stay in the East End, not with him after me. So I took off. I lived on the streets for a while, doin' what I could to survive, gettin' day work and things like that. But my luck run out and I got pneumonia. In a way, it turned out to be the best thing that ever happened to me. I collapsed on Inspector Witherspoon's doorstep." She looked up at his face. "You know the rest. I've been here ever since. I never thought I'd lay eyes on Raymond Skegit again."

Smythe got up and came around the table. He put his hand on her shoulder. "Don't worry, Betsy," he promised, his own voice none too steady and he was glad of the dim light. His own eyes were wet from hearing of her pain and suffering. "Nothing's going to happen to you. Raymond Skegit will never bother you again. I'll see to that."

CHAPTER 10

———◇◆◇◆◇———

"I've got to remember to stop in at the post office on my next day out," Betsy said to nobody in particular at breakfast the next morning. "I hope this case is finished by then."

"That's a good idea," Mrs. Jeffries replied absently. She barely heard what anyone said this morning. Her mind was preoccupied trying to sort out all the different pieces of the puzzle.

Somehow, she didn't think Grady Whitelaw was behind the murders. It didn't feel right. She had a sense that she was missing something, something so very apparent that if they weren't right in the middle of things, she'd see it in an instant.

"We can stop in on our way to the Zoological Gardens," Smythe said. "If this ruddy case is done by then."

"I don't think it'll ever be finished," Mrs. Goodge announced glumly. "Unless, of course, we find absolute proof that Grady Whitelaw is the killer, and in my opinion, he jolly well is. He had reason and his alibis are comin' apart faster than a chicken that's been cooked too long.''

Surprised, Betsy stared at the coachman. Despite his words the other day, there was one part of her that thought he wouldn't want to have anything to do with her. ''You still want me to go with you?'' she asked Smythe.

''Why wouldn't 'e want you to go?'' Wiggins asked. He thumped his crutch against the floor as he flopped down in his seat. ''Everyone likes the Zoological Gardens. I've a mind to go, too. I like lookin' at animals. Right educational, it is. Mind you, it's not as good as havin' a whole day at Mudies Lendin' Library.''

Smythe glared at him. He could hardly announce that he wanted time alone with Betsy, that he wanted to court her properly. ''Corse I want us to go,'' he said, turning his attention to the maid. ''It'da be a nice day out. I said we would, didn't I?''

''When we goin', then?'' Wiggins asked cheerfully.

''You can't go, Wiggins,'' Betsy said. She grinned at Smythe. ''You'd never be able to hobble around the zoo on them crutches.''

''Why don't you wait till I'm off the ruddy things?'' he asked. ''Then we could all go together, make a day of it.

'' 'Cause they want to go by themselves,'' Mrs. Goodge interjected. ''They'd like to be alone.''

Wiggins's jaw dropped open. He stared first at Betsy, who was staring at the toe of her shoe, then at Smythe, who stared right back at him. ''Well, I never. So that's the way the wind blows, is it? No one ever tells me what's goin' on round 'ere.''

''I don't think Smythe's and Betsy's private business is

any of your concern," Mrs. Goodge retorted. "Anyway, we'd best get this murder solved before we make any plans. Come on, everyone, finish your breakfast. I've got some sources comin' in here this morning and I need this kitchen empty."

"But you just said you thought Whitelaw was the killer," Wiggins complained. He hated being rushed through his meal. "So what's the ruddy 'urry?"

"We don't know who the killer is," the cook shot back. "And we don't stop lookin' just because we've got us a good suspect. Isn't that right, Mrs. Jeffries?"

"What? Oh yes," Mrs. Jeffries said hastily. "That's frequently a mistake the police make. They think someone is guilty so they stop investigating."

They did as they were told. Wiggins hobbled out to the street to flag down a hansom, Smythe took off on some mysterious errand of his own after getting Betsy to promise she'd be careful, and Mrs. Jeffries went out into the gardens to have a good, long think.

Naturally, Mrs. Jeffries hadn't been outside more than five minutes before Lady Cannonberry cornered her.

"I saw you from my bedroom window," Ruth said breathlessly, as though she'd dashed out in a hurry, "and I simply had to tell you what I'd found out."

"Do sit down and take a breath," Mrs. Jeffries advised. Oh, well, she thought, it wasn't as though her thinking was doing any good. She still couldn't quite grasp what it was about this case that was eluding her. She patted the wooden bench beside her. "Do sit down."

Ruth shook her head. "I mustn't. I've a thousand things to do today. But I wanted you to know that I'm still work-

ing on 'our case.' I had another chat with Marisole yesterday after I spoke to you, and she told me ever so much
more.''

"How very resourceful of you," Mrs. Jeffries replied.

"Perhaps I will sit down," Ruth murmured. "I don't
think the dressmaker will mind if I'm a few minutes late,
and Gerald's good name is far more important than a ball
gown." She sat down next to the housekeeper. "Well, before I forget, I did find out something about Rosalind
Frampton. Not only was she an actress, but she was engaged to another man when she met George Frampton. She
broke off the engagement, though, and the poor fellow, it
was an actor, I believe, got so annoyed, he publicly made
a scene. Called her all sorts of names when she was dining
with George Frampton at a restaurant on the Strand. It was
quite a scandal. Frampton threaten to sue the man. But he
didn't, he got him sacked instead. Disgusting what people
with money can do, isn't it? That poor actor had a perfect
right to state his piece. Mind you, I don't approve of making scenes. But . . .''

Mrs. Jeffries wanted to avoid another diatribe on the evils
of class system. Not that she didn't agree with Lady Cannonberry on that particular issue, she did. But once Ruth
got started, she often wandered off the point. And Mrs.
Jeffries had an awful feeling they were running out of time.
"Did you find out the actor's name?"

"Nicholas Osborne." She frowned. "No, that's wrong.
That's the name of the poor child who went to that school
in Abingdon with Hornsley and Frampton. Oh, now I remember, the actor's name was Oswald. Morton Oswald.
But he left for the continent after Frampton got him sacked.

Pity, too. I hear he was quite a good actor. Poor fellow. I don't see what an English actor can do on the continent. Unless, of course, he can act in a foreign language. Do you think there are many actors that speak German or Italian?''

Something rang a bell in the back of Mrs. Jeffries's mind, but it was gone before she could catch it. "I've no idea. What else did you learn?"

"Not much, really. Marisole couldn't get her husband to talk much about Packards. It was quite a horrid school. I don't think he was very happy there."

"Packards?"

"Why, yes, that's where they all went to school. Hornsley, Frampton, and Whitelaw. Marisole's husband too. It's quite a ghastly place."

Packards. Mrs. Jeffries couldn't believe she'd been such a fool. Packards. Abingdon. Notes. Schoolboy pranks. She jumped up. "What day is it?" she cried.

"March fifteenth," Ruth exclaimed, gazing at her curiously. "Why? Have you forgotten an important engagement?"

"I've been such an idiot! How could I not see the pattern?"

Ruth stood up as well, her expression concerned. "Is something wrong?"

"Ruth, can you get over to Marisole's and find out something for me? It's rather urgent. It could be the key to this whole case."

"Of course I can. The dressmaker can wait. What do you want me to find out?"

*   *   *

Luty and Hatchet arrived as soon as they'd received Mrs. Jeffries's urgent summons. But by the time everyone was back, it was getting dark.

"Isn't the inspector back yet?" Mrs. Jeffries asked for the tenth time.

"No, he's still out," Mrs. Goodge replied. "He's gone for another of them walks. Can't think why he can't walk in the daytime like the rest of us. Why does he want to go out on these silly evening jaunts?"

Betsy came rushing into the kitchen. "Is Smythe back yet?" she asked, taking off her bonnet and hurling it toward the coat tree.

"Not yet," Mrs. Jeffries replied. "He's been gone all day. Did you find out anything?"

"You were right," Betsy cried. "I caught the maid just as she was leaving the house. He's packin' for a trip, all right. He's leavin' tonight on the ten o'clock from Paddington."

"And the rest?"

Betsy shook her head. "It's all true."

"What's goin' on here?" Luty demanded.

"Mrs. Jeffries has figured out who the real killer is," Wiggins said excitedly.

"And if we don't move quickly, he's going to kill again tonight." Mrs. Jeffries rushed over to the kitchen window and peeked out again. "Oh, where is Smythe? Where's the inspector?"

Smythe, whistling tunelessly but cheerfully, came through the back door. "Evenin' everyone," he called.

Mrs. Jeffries whirled around. "Smythe, thank goodness you're back. Have you seen the inspector?"

"I just now passed him. He were 'eadin' for the omnibus stop."

"Hurry," she ordered. "Go after him. It's a matter of life and death."

Smythe didn't ask any questions, he turned and ran for the back door.

"Hatchet, is the carriage outside?"

"Course it is," Luty answered. "We didn't fly over here."

"Good. Then can you go and fetch Constable Barnes?" She checked the clock on the mantel and did some quick mental calculations. "He should be about ready to go home now. If you're lucky, you can catch him at the Ladbroke Grove police station. Either there, or at home."

"And what shall I tell him, madam?" Hatchet put his hat back on and was striding toward the door as he spoke. He, too, sensed the urgency of the situation.

"Tell him to come here. Tell him that Inspector Witherspoon thinks he knows who the killer is and that he needs his help to stop another murder from being committed."

Mrs. Jeffries would never forgive herself if they were too late, if another person lost their life because she'd so desperately wanted Inspector Witherspoon to get the credit for this case that she'd waited too long.

"Excuse me, Hepzibah," Luty sputtered, "but would you mind tellin' me what in the dickens is goin' on here?"

"I say, are you certain of this?" Inspector Witherspoon asked Betsy.

"I got it straight from the maid, and she were the one packin' up his clothes."

He nodded slowly. He wasn't sure he quite understood just what was going on, but he thought it better to act than to risk another murder. Mind you, he told himself, if he was wrong, he'd find himself back in the records room instead of out solving homicides. He was rather surprised to find that idea depressing. Gracious, in the past two and a half years there had been times when he'd wanted to go back to his old job. "And you're quite certain of your information?" he asked Mrs. Jeffries.

"Yes, sir."

"Well, then, I guess I'd better get cracking." He started for the back stairs.

Mrs. Jeffries stopped him. "Excuse me, sir," she said, keeping one eye on the clock as she spoke. "But as Luty and Hatchet had dropped by, I took the liberty of asking Hatchet to fetch Constable Barnes. They should be here any minute."

"Excellent, Mrs. Jeffries. Excellent." Witherspoon was no coward, but he wasn't a fool either. If he was going to arrest a murderer, he would like to have Barnes there to assist him. "But I'm wondering if we should send a message to Inspector Nivens . . ."

"No!" shouted Mrs. Jeffries, Betsy, Mrs. Goodge, and even Luty at the same time.

"There isn't time, sir," Mrs. Jeffries said quickly. From outside she heard the sound of a carriage pulling up.

A moment later, Hatchet, followed by a surprised-looking Constable Barnes, came in the back door.

"I'm so glad you're here, Constable," Witherspoon said. "Er, by the way, where is Inspector Nivens . . .?" Really, he must at least try and bring the inspector in on this. It would be most unfair if he didn't.

"Inspector Nivens left the station early today," Barnes replied, looking pleased as punch about the situation. "He was havin' dinner with some politician over in Fulham. Told me not to bother him till morning."

"Sir," Mrs. Jeffries said urgently, "you really must get going."

"Yes, yes, of course. Come along Barnes," Witherspoon started for the door. "I'd like you to accompany me."

"Maybe I ought to come along as well," Smythe suggested, "seein' as 'ow Inspector Nivens isn't 'ere."

Witherspoon paused. He really should stop and bring along some more police constables. But there really wasn't time. And Smythe was a sensible chap. He wouldn't do anything foolish or dangerous. "I think that's a splendid idea. Thank you, Smythe. But mind you, I won't have you put yourself in any danger. You must take care to do as I say at all times."

Confused, Barnes looked from the inspector to the coachman. "Where are we goin', sir?"

Witherspoon popped his bowler on his head. "We're going to catch a killer, Constable Barnes."

"Are you sure of all this, sir?" Barnes asked as the carriage came to a halt in front of the house. "I mean, it's pure supposition, sir. If we're wrong . . ."

"If we're wrong, I'll end up in the records room and you'll end up walkin' a beat in Shoreditch," said Witherspoon with a shrug. "I quite understand if you'd like to disassociate yourself from my actions. After all, it's not even my case.''

"I'm goin' in with you, sir,'' Barnes said firmly. "I've confidence you know what you're doin'.''

"Thank you. I appreciate your faith in me, Barnes.'' Witherspoon hoped the constable's faith wasn't misplaced. "And do remember, if I'm right, we may very well be saving a man's life.''

"I think I'd better come in with ya, too,'' Smythe said. He was staring at the house. Except for a flare of brightness from the fanlight over the door, the place was in darkness. The hairs on the back of his neck stood straight up, a sure sign that something bad was about to happen. "I don't much like the look of this.''

Witherspoon hesitated. It was one thing for he and Barnes to face a murderer, but it was quite another to ask his coachman to risk his life. On the other hand, Smythe had come in quite useful a time or two in the past. "Uh, why don't you come as far as the door? That way, you can be at the ready if someone has to run and get help.''

They moved out of the carriage and up the dark walkway. Witherspoon reached the door first. He raised his hand to knock, but the door was unlatched and standing open a couple of inches. He pushed inside, with Constable Barnes right on his heels.

It took a moment for his eyes to adjust to the light. But when they did, he gasped in surprise.

Grady Whitelaw, on his knees in front of the staircase and holding a hand to his head, moaned softly. Blood spurted from between his fingers and a loose tie dangled from around his neck. He pointed toward an open doorway on the other side of the staircase. "He's getting away. Heard you coming and ran."

There was the sound of breaking glass. Barnes and Witherspoon dashed forward and flew into the drawing room in time to see a man wearing a heavy overcoat and a bowler hat climbing out of the window.

"Halt in the name of the law!" Witherspoon cried.

But the man kept right on going.

"Is 'e goin' to be all right?" Smythe asked anxiously. He'd come running in as soon as he'd heard Witherspoon's yells.

"He's bleedin' badly, but the wound don't look too deep," Barnes replied. "Mr. Whitelaw, are you able to sit up?"

Whitelaw moaned but gamely tried to sit up. "I let him in," he said softly. "I thought it was the police."

"Where are your servants?" Barnes asked.

"Out," Whitelaw mumbled. He slumped down on his elbow. "I gave them the evening off to go to George's wake. I was on my way there myself when the inspector came . . . he said my life was in danger . . ." His eyes closed.

"Is he dead?" Witherspoon asked anxiously.

Barnes felt for a pulse. "He's unconscious, but he needs a doctor."

"Best leave him layin' where 'e is," said Smythe, helping the wounded man back onto the floor. "I'll nip up to the corner. There's a constable on patrol there. We need some 'elp 'ere."

"Hurry, Smythe," Witherspoon urged as the coachman

took off at a dead run for the front door. "We've no time to lose. Otherwise the miscreant will get away."

"You mean you know who he is?" Barnes asked.

"Indeed I do," Witherspoon replied. He sincerely hoped that his conclusions, or rather the conclusions he'd come to with the help of the staff, were correct. But even if they were wrong, they'd at least been in time to save Grady Whitelaw's life.

Smythe must have run all the way to the corner and made the constable run too, for they were back in just a few moments. Witherspoon briefly explained what had happened, while Barnes went out and summoned a doctor.

They left Whitelaw with the constable and the doctor. As soon as they were back in the carriage, Barnes asked, "Where to now, sir? The Yard?"

"Oh no, we've got to make an arrest." He stuck his head out the window and yelled at Smythe, "How quickly can you get us to Mayfair?"

Again, they pulled up in front of a darkened house. This time, when Smythe asked if he should come in with the inspector, Witherspoon didn't hesitate. "If you wouldn't mind, Smythe. That would be a great help. But do stay near the front door in case there's trouble. We may need you to dash out again and find some more constables."

They walked up to the front door. Witherspoon banged the knocker and yelled, "Open up in the name of the law!" But he needn't have bothered. Like Whitelaw's house, this door swung open, too.

Taking a deep breath, the inspector pushed his way inside. The lights were dim, but the house wasn't in total darkness. "I say," the inspector called, "is anyone here?"

"There should be servants, sir," Barnes said uneasily. "This is a rich man's house."

"Yes, well, I don't expect there are any servants about the place tonight," said Witherspoon as he started down the hallway, past a staircase and a table with a large potted fern, to what he hoped was a drawing room or study at the far end of the passage. "I expect he's given them the evening off."

"To go to Frampton's wake?" Barnes suggested. He didn't like this, he didn't like it at all. The place was too quiet.

"No. I don't think our killer will be sending any of his servants to pay their respects to either of the victims."

"You're absolutely right, inspector," said a voice quietly from behind them. "It will be a cold day in the pits of Hades before anyone in my employ pays their respects to those animals."

They whirled about. A man wearing a heavy overcoat, bowler hat, and a pair of spectacles stood at the foot of the staircase. He was holding a revolver in his hand.

Witherspoon's heart leapt into his throat. "Now, there's no need for that."

The man looked at the revolver and smiled. "You're right about that too, sir. There isn't." He put the revolver down on the table next to a potted fern. "I'm not going to shoot you. I don't kill innocent people."

Witherspoon was rather stunned. He wasn't quite sure what to do now. So he did precisely what the law required.

"Justin Vincent," he said formally, "you're under arrest for the murders of Peter Hornsley and George Frampton."

"Haven't you forgotten about the attempted murder of Grady Whitelaw?" Vincent asked easily. "Or did I hit him hard enough to kill him before you so rudely interrupted me?"

"He's still alive," Barnes said. "But maybe not for long."

Smythe, who'd been watching the whole proceedings with his jaw hanging open, edged toward the front door. Like it or not, he was goin' for help. This was too much for the inspector to handle.

But Vincent saw the coachman move. He snatched up the gun and pointed it right at his chest. "I wouldn't do that if I were you." Smythe stopped.

"I don't want to kill an innocent person," Vincent continued softly. "But I will if I have to."

Witherspoon blanched. He didn't mind if Vincent pointed a gun at him, but he wasn't having the man threaten his coachman. "Now see here," he started for Vincent.

"Don't move another step, Inspector," Vincent said, "or I'll shoot your man right where he stands."

"What do you want?" Witherspoon cried. "You must know you won't get away with this."

"I don't want to get away with it," said Vincent, smiling. "All I want is for all of you to come into the drawing room. I'd like to make a full confession. Your constable there"—he nodded at Barnes—"can write it down for me."

Witherspoon didn't see that he had much choice. "All right, but I must insist you let my coachman go."

Vincent thought about it for a moment. "All right, there's no harm in letting him leave. By the time he gets back with help, it will all be over."

Witherspoon nodded to Smythe.

The coachman hesitated. He didn't like leavin' the inspector with a madman—especially a madman with a gun.

"Go on," Witherspoon urged. "Go and get help."

Smythe had no choice. He turned and hurried out the front door.

As soon as he was gone, Vincent gestured with the gun toward the open door at the end of the hallway. "Let's step into the drawing room, Inspector. We'll be far more comfortable there."

They did as he asked. There was a cheerful fire in the hearth next to the desk. A leather settee and a small table with a red fringed shawl was next to it. There were various other pieces of furniture scattered about the room, but the inspector was too busy staring at the gun in Vincent's possession to admire the decor.

Vincent motioned for Barnes to sit behind the desk. "There's paper and a pen there, Constable," he said conversationally, as though he were inviting Barnes to help himself to tea and cakes. "Make sure you listen carefully and take down everything I say. I want this read at the inquest."

Barnes, his face pale, but his expression determined, did as he was told.

"Mr. Vincent," Witherspoon began. He was the senior policeman here. It was his duty to take charge of the situation. Only how did one take charge when the other fellow had a weapon and you didn't?

"Oh, do sit down, Inspector," said Vincent, waving the gun at the settee. "This is going to take a few moments. You'll be much more comfortable sitting than standing."

Witherspoon sat. "I take it you would like to confess."

Vincent walked over and poured himself a glass of whiskey from the bottle on a teak table by the window. "Would either of you like a drink?"

"No, thank you, I'm on duty," the inspector said.

Barnes shook his head.

"Well, then, I do hope you don't mind if I do." He took a long drink of his whiskey, and grimaced. "In answer to your question, Inspector, yes, I'm going to make a full confession. But I will do it in my own words. I want the whole world to know what kind of men I killed." He filled the glass again. "And I want your word of honor that my statement will be read at the inquest."

"You're hardly in a position to bargain, Mr. Vincent," Witherspoon retorted.

"Oh, but I am." Vincent smiled. "I've got the gun."

"Yes, quite. I do see your point."

"Your word, Inspector," said Vincent, raising the gun and leveling it at Barnes. "I'm an excellent shot, sir. I learned how to use firearms in America. Los Angeles, to be exact."

"You have my word, sir," Witherspoon sputtered, as he watched his constable turn even paler. "But there won't be an inquest, sir. There will be a trial."

"I doubt that, Inspector. But let's not quibble over details. Whether it's a trial or an inquest, I want my statement read. Is that clear?"

"Perfectly."

Satisfied, Vincent nodded. "Take this down, Constable." He took another swig of the whiskey. "I, Justin Vincent, born Nicholas Osborne, freely admit that I murdered Peter Hornsley and George Frampton. I freely admit that I also attempted to murder Grady Whitelaw. I did this while in full possession . . ."

"Would you mind slowin' down a bit, sir?" Barnes interrupted. "I'm not that fast a writer. Now, how do you spell 'possession'?"

"P-o-s—" Witherspoon started to spell the word.

"Oh, for God's sake, just do the best that you can," Vincent cried. "May I continue?"

Barnes nodded.

"I did this while in full possession of my faculties and with malice aforethought." He broke off and grinned. "That's an American legal expression. Do they have it over here as well? I rather like it though, don't you, Inspector? *Malice*. It's such a good word, and so descriptive. It says precisely what I felt."

"You had a grudge against the victims?" Witherspoon asked.

Vincent laughed. "Grudge? That's hardly what I would call it. Those despicable bullies ruined my life. They were responsible for my mother's death and sent me into exile."

"How very unfortunate."

"It was a bit more than 'unfortunate,' Inspector," Vincent said softly. He put the glass down and pulled off the black leather glove on his right hand. He held his hand up. "Do you see this?"

Witherspoon leaned closer, his eyes straining to see in the faint light. A huge dark scar covered the back of the hand, the thumb, and several of the fingers. "That looks like you've been burned, sir."

"Hornsley held my hand in a fire when I was eleven years old. Frampton held me down and Whitelaw kept watch." Still holding the gun, he stared at his own hand. "I was small for my age. They were sixteen. Hornsley was the ringleader. They called themselves the Conquerors. That was the name of their little group at that wretched school my uncle sent me to. It was a horrid place. A place no one should send a child to."

"Why did they do it, sir?" Barnes asked.

"Because I wouldn't allow them to use me," Vincent said bluntly. "I was small for my age, quite pretty, or so I was told. Hornsley thought he could do with me as he liked, but I refused to cooperate. I was small, but more than capable of putting up a good fight. That's when the bullying started. They made my life miserable. Stole my pens, poured ink on my clothing, they did everything possible to make everyone hate me, and, what's worse, they succeeded."

"Didn't anyone notice the burn on your hand?" Witherspoon asked.

"Of course they did." Vincent laughed. "But they lied about that as well, claimed that I'd burned myself by falling into the fire. That's when I told on them, you see. That's when I told the headmaster that Hornsley was a pederast. But the odd thing was, the headmaster didn't want to know. No one wanted to know. Not the teachers or the prefects or the parents. Everyone looked the other way and advised me not to make trouble."

"So you left the school?" guessed Witherspoon. Really,

he should think Vincent had been glad to get away from such an awful place.

"Oh no, it wasn't that simple, Inspector. I didn't get a chance to leave. I was expelled for stealing. The Conquerors had the Latin master in their pockets, you see. Hornsley had been indulging in unnatural practices with Hickstrom for years. The old sodomite would do anything Hornsley wanted. He deliberately claimed I'd stolen his watch. So I was the one that was expelled. I was the one sent home in disgrace. I was the one who watched my mother throw herself in the Thames after my uncle threw us out of his house because I'd ruined the family name." He smiled bitterly. "But the Latin master's dead, too. I took care of Hickstrom first. Poor old fellow toppled off a bridge and into an icy river. I stood and watched him drown. Fitting, isn't it?"

Witherspoon was so stunned by this he couldn't think of a thing to say. Vincent, apparently, didn't expect him to say anything.

"I've spent thirty years planning their deaths," Vincent said slowly. He picked up the glass off the table and drained it. "Thirty years, Inspector."

"Why did you use my name?"

"I'm sorry about that," Vincent said. "But you see, I wanted to make sure that you weren't given this case. I'm not a fool. I've followed your cases in the papers. You've solved some very difficult murders. And you've solved them brilliantly. I didn't want the inspector who'd cracked those horrible Kensington High Street murders snooping about on this case, so I used your name. Silly, really. I oughtn't to have done anything."

"Did you plant that note on George Frampton?" the inspector asked. "The one signed with my name."

"Yes," Vincent admitted. "A miscalculation on my part. Obviously, you took exception to my masquerade. I'd been rather hoping you'd be sent off to the country by the powers that be. Besides, as a policeman I could gain access to my victims so very easily. If you say you're from Scotland Yard, people will unlock their doors and let you right inside." He sighed. "It's a pity about Whitelaw, I did so want him dead, too."

Vincent suddenly started to sway. "Did you get this all down, Constable?" he demanded.

"Yes, sir, most of it." Barnes looked up from his paper. "Are you all right, sir?"

"I'm fine——" but Vincent didn't complete the sentence. The gun slipped from his hand and he collapsed onto the floor.

Witherspoon rushed over to him. He knelt down beside him. "Mr. Vincent," he said urgently, "we must get you to hospital."

"It's too late," Vincent whispered. He tried to raise his head. "But you'll make sure my statement is read at the inquest?"

"It will be read," said Witherspoon as he tucked his arm under Vincent's head, protecting it from the floor. "I promise you, it will be read."

"Thank you," Vincent rasped. "I'm sorry I used your name, I didn't mean to . . ."

"Please," the inspector begged, "don't try and speak anymore. Help is on the way. We'll get you to hospital."

"Too late . . . poison . . ." With that, he closed his eyes and died.

"Inspector, Inspector Witherspoon," cried out Smythe, his voice frantic, and a rush of footsteps sounded in the hallway.

"In here," Barnes called as he charged out from behind the desk.

Smythe, accompanied by what looked like a battalion of uniformed police, charged into the room. He skidded to a halt at the sight of Justin Vincent lying on the carpet.

"He's dead," the inspector said softly.

" 'Ow?"

"He killed himself," said Witherspoon as he gently lowered the dead man to the carpet. He pointed to the bottle on the table. "Barnes, let's take that whiskey bottle into evidence. Mustn't leave something like that about. Someone might accidentally drink from it."

CHAPTER 11

"How did you figure it out?" Smythe asked. They were all gathered round the table at Upper Edmonton Gardens. Everyone, that is, except Constable Barnes and Inspector Witherspoon. They were still down at the station, explaining everything to a rather pleased Chief Inspector Curling and a furious Inspector Nivens.

"I almost didn't until it was too late," Mrs. Jeffries admitted. "You see, we'd all been looking at this case the wrong way."

"Wrong way?" Luty frowned. "Nell's bells, Hepzibah, I think we did pretty danged good."

"We did do good," Mrs. Jeffries laughed. "What I meant was that we all accepted a certain premise far too early in our investigations."

"You mean that the murders had something to do with the company and not with the victims?" Betsy said.

"That's right. It wasn't until Wiggins mentioned the Ides of March that I understood, and even that didn't do it until

Lady Cannonberry mentioned that name again—Nicholas Osborne, also known as Justin Vincent. Why, his very name should have given us a clue.''

"Yes, it should have," Hatchet agreed. "It means 'just conqueror' in Latin."

"Well, how in the dickens was we supposed to know that?" exclaimed Luty, who shot her butler a fierce frown.

"Let me start at the beginning," Mrs. Jeffries explained. "You see, from the very first the notes were important, but because they were difficult, because none of us could make any sense of them, we tended to ignore them."

"So did the police," Smythe added.

"True, but we're not the police. We should have seen what they meant."

"But like Luty says, none of us, except Hatchet, knows Latin," protested Betsy.

"I'm not talking about what the notes *said*, I'm talking about the act itself." Mrs. Jeffries threw her hands up. "The killer pinned a note to his victim's chest. What does that remind you of?"

"Pin the tail on the donkey," Wiggins suggested.

"Don't be daft, boy," Mrs. Goodge snapped.

"That's silly," Betsy said.

"He's absolutely right," Mrs. Jeffries interrupted. "That's precisely what it meant. The killer did something a silly schoolboy would have done. And none of us saw it."

Hatchet pursed his lips. "I'm not sure that it would have made any difference if we had realized the significance of the act."

"No, perhaps not," Mrs. Jeffries said. "But it might

have made us start thinking along different lines and asking different sorts of questions. Why, from the very beginning, there was an element of childish, schoolboy behavior about this case, but none of us saw it."

"What do you mean?" Wiggins asked. "I don't see nuthin' schoolboyish about killin' someone, and that's when this case started."

Mrs. Jeffries shook her head. "But it wasn't. The case started a month earlier than that. It started with the break-ins at the office building. But none of us even thought to pursue that line of inquiry. Fortunately, Smythe investigated and found that the office of Hornsley, Frampton, and Whitelaw was the only one broken into. As soon as he told us that nothing had been stolen from the office and that, really, the only harm done was a few broken pens and some ink poured on Hornsley's desk, we should have seen the connection. But we didn't. We were already too committed to another, wrong idea about the crime. Let this be a lesson to us. From now on, we form no opinions until we have all the facts."

"I see what you mean," Hatchet said thoughtfully. "The break-in wasn't really a break-in. It was just the sort of thing that silly boys do when they think they can get away with it. Something to torment and inconvenience, but no real harm meant."

"Seems to me there was plenty of harm done," Luty snapped. She was annoyed at Hatchet for seeming to get the point faster than she had. "There were two men murdered."

"But that break-in was almost like Vincent was tryin' to warn his victims," Betsy pointed out.

"I think he was," Mrs. Jeffries stated flatly. "I think he was trying, in his own sick way, to give them fair warning. But they couldn't see it, either."

"I still don't see how you figured it out," Mrs. Goodge complained. "I'm still muddled up about it."

"It was several things, actually. All along I had the sense that there was something right under my nose and I couldn't for the life of me see what it was," Mrs. Jeffries said. "But nothing fell into place until this morning when I was talking to Lady Cannonberry. She mentioned Nicholas Osborne, but, more importantly, she mentioned that Hornsley, Frampton, and Whitelaw had gone to school in Abingdon. Then I remembered where I'd heard that name before." She smiled at Betsy. "Vincent's maid had told Betsy that Vincent had gone to school there as well. I knew it couldn't be a coincidence. Then I came in here and looked at the calendar. The first murder happened on the ninth, the second on the twelfth, and then I knew. Vincent was going to kill Whitelaw tonight—the Ides of March— March fifteenth. Children are very much taken with ritual; three is almost a magic number to them."

Luty snorted. "Vincent's no child. The man's got to be at least forty."

"But he was acting out a child's fantasy," Mrs. Jeffries pointed out. "At least that's what I thought he was doing. But it all added up. Lady Cannonberry said Osborne's hand was burned. Justin Vincent always wore gloves."

"So that's why you sent me over to his house to see what he was up to," Betsy exclaimed. "You was certain even then what he was up to." She gave Smythe an impudent smile. "Turns out that clue was important, doesn't it?"

Smythe frowned at her. "You left the 'ouse this afternoon?"

"I took a hansom," Betsy protested. "And I was careful. Besides, I did find out that Vincent had let all his servants go and was planning on leaving town tonight."

Mrs. Jeffries glanced from the maid to the coachman. She wondered what was going on. But now wasn't the time to bring up the subject. "That was when I knew for certain," she said.

"Mind you, he did give them all six months' wages," Betsy said. "So he couldn't have been too bad a person."

"Was that all that made it drop into place?" Luty asked. "Just those piddly little clues?"

"No, there were a number of things. First of all, I remembered Constable Barnes telling us that Vincent had never met the other partners. All the negotiations to buy into the firm had been done through solicitors and through Grady Whitelaw. I thought that odd. Surely, if he was spending a great deal of money, Vincent would have wanted to meet with all the principals in the company. Yet he didn't. Why? Because I think he was planning on killing Hornsley and Frampton first, and he didn't want them to recognize him as their new partner. He didn't care if Whitelaw recognized him, he was going to kill him last, so I expect he thought it didn't matter."

"But he was disguisin' himself as the inspector," Betsy protested. She'd rather liked Vincent. "So how could Hornsley and Frampton have recognized him?"

"No disguise is that good, girl," Luty said. "And remember, he had to get close enough to cosh them on the head and strangle them.''

"I think you're right," Smythe agreed. "I do think he planned the order of the murders. I read the statement he dictated to Barnes. Hornsley was the one that held his 'and to the fire, Frampton 'eld him down, and Whitelaw kept watch. He killed the ringleader first. Killed the one that had hurt him the worst first.''

"Can't say that I much blame 'im," Luty said. "Only I wouldn't have waited thirty years to get even. Imagine doin' that to a little boy.''

"But that's no reason for murder," Wiggins protested. "It's one thing to want a bit of revenge, but 'e didn't 'ave to kill 'em.''

"I can't imagine carryin' a grudge for that long," Mrs. Goodge said. "You'd think Vincent would have forgotten as he grew up.''

"Some people never forget," Betsy said. She shivered and crossed her arms over her chest. Smythe knew she was thinking of her own brush with the past.

He tried to catch her eye, but she was looking away from him, staring at the clock as though she could will time to run backward. But he was being fanciful. Maybe she was just tired.

Inspector Witherspoon arrived home before they finished their meeting. "I say," he said, "I was rather hoping you'd all be up.''

"We wanted to hear what happened, sir," Mrs. Jeffries explained. "Luty and Hatchet decided to stay, too.''

"I couldn't leave without knowin'," Luty explained

hastily. "And Hatchet here wouldn't sleep a wink all night if he didn't find out how things turned out."

Hatchet contented himself with a quick glare. He didn't wish to spar with his employer in front of the inspector.

Despite his jovial manner, they could all see the evening's events had taken a toll on their inspector. He was quite pale, his hair was sticking up on end, as though he'd been running his hands through it, and his fingers shook as he took the cup of tea Mrs. Jeffries poured for him.

"It was quite dreadful, really," he murmured. "Vincent, or I should say Osborne, is dead. He took poison; it was in a bottle of whiskey. It was quite deliberate, I'm sure. I think he'd planned on killing himself all along."

"What kind did 'e take?" Wiggins asked curiously.

"We're not sure. The police surgeon thinks it might have been some sort of plant poison, but he won't know for certain till he does the postmortem. It's certainly something we're not familiar with in England. It wasn't arsenic or strychnine—Vincent died far too quickly for either of those. But Dr. Bosworth happened by and he said that there are a variety of poisonous substances derived from plants in America. We're thinking it could be one of those."

"Gracious, sir, how very awful for you," Mrs. Jeffries said.

"Watching a man die is rather terrible, even if he is a murderer." Witherspoon closed his eyes briefly. "I don't think I shall ever forget it."

"What I don't understand is how he committed the murders," Mrs. Goodge said. "He had an alibi for both of them. Was his servants lying about him supposedly bein' at home?"

"No," Witherspoon explained. "They weren't. But you see, he'd given strict instructions not to be disturbed when he was working. That's why he ate his dinner so early. He'd then tell the staff he was working, pop into his study, put on his disguise, slip out through a small door that most of the servants didn't even realize was there, commit the murder, and come back in the same way. It was very clever. Very clever, indeed. But then, it should have been. He'd been planning his crimes for a long time; that much became obvious when we searched his house."

"What did you find?" Hatchet asked.

Witherspoon toyed with his cup. "We found the disguise he wore, of course. He kept that under his bed in a carpet bag. He even had a fake mustache and wig."

"That must have been the one Martha saw him with," Betsy exclaimed. "She thought he had a lock of his sweetheart's hair."

"Well, that was not a lock of anyone's hair, it was a fake mustache from Herringer and Sons, Wigmakers."

"There's something I don't understand," Wiggins said.

"And what's that?" the inspector replied.

"Well, accordin' to what we know, Vincent didn't ask the partners to let 'im buy into the company. The partners come to 'im. If 'e was plannin' on these murders, why'd he want to go into business with 'em?"

"I think I know," Mrs. Jeffries said thoughtfully. "I think he wanted to watch them suffer. I think he wanted to watch Frampton and Whitelaw fall apart, and then he wanted to kill them."

"I agree," Witherspoon said. "He also wanted to be part of it, too. As a partner, he'd be right in the thick of it. As to their coming to him, instead of the other way round, I think he knew exactly how to manipulate them. Vincent had complete dossiers on the three partners. We found them in his desk. He'd hired a firm of private detectives to watch them. He knew all about their business, their private lives, everything. He even had notes regarding their intention to expand the business. So I suspect that approaching their rival, Damon Hilliard, was all part of his plan."

"Where'd he get his money?" Betsy asked.

"He did very well in land speculation in California," Witherspoon replied. "Actually, he'd made a fortune."

"What a waste of a life." Amazed, Betsy shook her head. "He had all that money and all he wanted to do was kill the boys that had bullied him when he was a school-boy."

"The sins of the past, Betsy," Witherspoon shrugged philosophically.

Smythe didn't want the conversation to continue in that vein. Betsy's past was over and done with, he'd seen to that. "Is Mr. Whitelaw goin' to be all right?" he asked.

"He'll be fine. He's a mild concussion but nothing a few days of rest won't cure." Witherspoon sighed. "Mind you, I think he's quite lucky."

"He is indeed, sir," Mrs. Jeffries said bluntly. "If you hadn't figured out who the real killer was in time, he'd be dead like the others."

Witherspoon smiled sheepishly. "Come now, Mrs. Jeffries, I can hardly take credit for solving this case."

"Oh, but you can, sir," she insisted. "The only thing we'd determined was that there would be another killing tonight. You were the one that concluded who the killer must be and who his intended victim was." This wasn't precisely true, but Mrs. Jeffries didn't want the inspector to realize it.

"If you'll recall, sir," she continued when he opened his mouth to protest, "the only thing I told you when you came in this evening was that the murders had occurred three days apart. After we discussed the matter for a few moments and I told you what Betsy had found out this afternoon, about Vincent getting ready to leave, you figured out the rest." This statement wasn't true either, but she thought it best to convince him that it was. When Smythe had brought the inspector back this evening, she'd carefully fed him the information he needed to come to the right conclusion.

In the past, she'd observed that people would frequently forget the circumstances of an event and then take all the credit once the deed was accomplished. This trait was especially common in men. Even her dear late husband, who'd been a constable with the Yorkshire police, had been prone to this peculiarity of character. But Mrs. Jeffries didn't mind. It didn't really matter whether or not she and the staff got any credit for helping. What was important to all of them was that they could continue to help. Furthermore, if they wanted to keep on detecting without interference, she'd better convince the inspector it was he who'd solved the case, not them.

Witherspoon considered her words. "Why, I do believe you're right, Mrs. Jeffries. Gracious, perhaps I'm a better detective than I'd thought."

*   *   *

At eleven o'clock, Smythe slipped out the back door and into the garden. He paused, giving his eyes time to adjust to the darkness. Directly ahead of him a match struck. Smythe walked toward the sudden flare of light.

Blimpey Groggins, puffing on a cigar, came out from under the huge oak tree. "Evenin', Smythe, you're right on time."

"Is it done?"

"It's done," Blimpey grinned around his cigar. "Funniest job I ever pulled, a right ole lark it was."

"Any trouble gettin' in?"

"Nah, Skegit's locks were so flimsy a three-year-old could skiffle 'em."

"Did you leave the stuff?"

Blimpey chuckled. "Raymond Skegit should be gettin' a visit from Her Majesty's excise boys in less than an hour. He'll be right startled, Raymond will. Probably spend the next ten years wonderin' 'ow they got on to 'im."

"That'll be our little secret," Smythe said. "You done good, Blimpey. I owe ya for this."

"And you'll pay, me friend, you'll pay." Blimpey laughed again, taken by his own wit. "But even if you couldn't pay, it would do me 'eart good to 'elp put someone like Skegit away. When the customs lads see everythin' we stashed in Raymond's room, they'll put 'im away for ten years. Governments might let you get away with murder. But smugglin', not payin' duty? They'll lock the bloke up and throw away the key."

"Good thing for me that you and your mates cottoned on to Skegit's second business," Smythe said, as he reached into his pocket and drew out a thick wad of notes.

"Otherwise, I was gonna 'ave to find another way to take care of Skegit."

"Wouldn't be no loss if he was put six feet under," Blimpey said. "Not many would mourn 'im, and, take me word for it, the peelers wouldn't look too 'ard to find who done it."

Smythe shook his head. He wanted Skegit out of the way so he couldn't harm Betsy, and thanks to Blimpey and his friends, he'd found a way to do it without resorting to violence. "I couldn't do murder," he said quietly, handing the bills to Blimpey. "Not even scum like Skegit. I'm glad the bastard dabbled in smugglin'. Makes it easier to get shut of 'im."

Blimpey clasped the roll of bills to his bosom. He didn't bother to count it. He knew Smythe was as good as his word. "Skegit *dabbled* in smugglin'. 'E'll be right narked when 'e realizes 'e's been set up. 'Ave you thought of that?"

"I'm not afraid of 'im," Smythe replied. "Besides, by the time 'e gets out, 'e'll be an old man. The kind of contraband your lot planted ought to get 'im a good sentence."

"It cost you plenty," Blimpey agreed. He cocked his chin to one side. "If you don't mind me askin', where you gettin' this kind of lolly?"

Smythe did mind him asking, but he didn't want to offend him either. Blimpey was a useful friend to have. "'Ere and there," he replied casually. "I've saved a bit over the years."

"On a coachman's pay?" Blimpey was clearly incredulous.

"I play the ponies, too," Smythe shrugged. "I'm good at it."

Blimpey raised the wad of notes to his mouth and kissed them. "And I'm glad of it, Smythe. You're a regular gent to do business with."

Smythe waited until Blimpey was out of the gardens before going back into the house. He hadn't liked what he'd had to do, but he couldn't think of any other way to handle Skegit. The man was a pimp and probably a murderer. God knew what he would do to Betsy if he ever got his hands on her. Smythe shuddered as he pulled open the back door. He didn't want to think about that. He didn't want to think of her in the clutches of that monster. Even though what he'd done wasn't exactly right, it weren't exactly wrong either. That's what he told himself as he hurried down the hallway and into the kitchen.

He skidded to a halt.

Betsy was sitting at the dining table.

"I was waiting for you," she said calmly. "I saw you slip down the stairs after everyone else had gone up."

"Oh." He ambled to the table, trying to appear as casual as possible.

"What was you doin' outside?"

"Gettin' a breath of air," he replied, dropping into the chair next to her.

She stared at him for a moment. "Who was that man you was—were—" she corrected, "talking with?"

Smythe wondered if he could bluff his way out of this. Then he decided against it. Betsy had shared her secrets with him, she deserved to have a few answers. But he couldn't resist teasing her. "Spyin' on me, were ya?" he asked, giving her his cockiest grin.

She didn't crack a smile. "No," she replied solemnly. "I was just curious when I saw you go out. I was goin' to come out myself and then I saw that other man out there."

"Well, if you must know . . ."

"I must."

"It was a fellow named Blimpey Groggins."

"I saw you give him something," she pressed. "What was it?"

"Nothing. Well, I give him a couple of quid 'cause 'e's skint and 'elps me every now and then."

"How much?"

"A couple of pounds is all," he lied. He didn't want her to know how much money he'd really paid Blimpey; otherwise, she'd feel beholden to him for life. "Look, Blimpey give me a 'and with Raymond Skegit . . ."

"Skegit," she cried. "Why are you messin' about with the likes of him?"

"I fixed it so 'e won't ever bother you again, lass," he said softly.

Her eyes widened in alarm. "What have you done, Smythe? Oh God, I don't want someone like him comin' after you," she cried. "I knew I shouldn't have told you the truth. I knew it."

"Now, don't upset yerself," he said, reaching over and patting her shoulder. "I didn't kill the man. All I did was fix it so 'e's . . ." he hesitated, wondering just how much to tell her.

"So he's what?" she demanded.

"So 'e's off the streets and not 'urtin' anyone," he finished. "By this time tomorrow night, Raymond Skegit will be sittin' inside a jail cell and hopin' 'e's got the money to pay a solicitor."

She opened her mouth but he shushed her by gently putting his fingers on her lips. "Don't ask me no more questions, lass. I did it for you and that's all ya need to know."

Stunned, she gazed at him. "I don't know what to say."

"Don't say anythin'," he ordered softly. "Just know that I'll do whatever I 'ave to to keep ya safe."

"You're a good friend, Smythe," she said, her eyes filling with tears. "No, that's not right," she leaned forward, her lips coming close to his. "You're much more than just a friend, Smythe."

"Hey," Wiggins called. His crutches thumped heavily down the stairs. "What's goin' on down 'ere? 'As there been another murder?"

Betsy jumped back and glanced guiltily at the stairs.

Smythe groaned in frustration. If Wiggins hadn't already had a sprained ankle, the coachman would be sorely tempted to hobble him.

Witherspoon reached for the pot of damson preserves Mrs. Jeffries had just put on the dining table. "I really mustn't dawdle over breakfast this morning. I've got to get to the Yard and write up my report."

Betsy stuck her head in the room. "Inspector Nivens is here to see you, sir."

"I'll announce myself," said a familiar voice, interrupting the maid. Nigel Nivens, his expression hard and grim, stepped into the room. "Well, what do you have to say for yourself, Witherspoon?" he demanded.

"Say for myself?"

"About stealing my case."

"Would you care for a cup of tea, Inspector Nivens?" Mrs. Jeffries smiled blandly.

"No, thank you. Well, Witherspoon, I'm waiting."

"I assure you, Inspector," Witherspoon said hastily, "that it was never my intention to 'steal your case,' as you so harshly put it."

"Then why didn't you make sure I made the arrest?" Nivens snapped.

"Constable Barnes said you were dining with a politician and mustn't be disturbed," Witherspoon tried to explain.

But Nivens refused to listen. "You've made me look like a fool, Witherspoon. And I'll not forget it." And with that, he turned on his heel and marched out of the room.

"Get out of my way, woman," they heard him yell. A moment later, the front door slammed.

"Who's he talking to?" Betsy asked curiously, looking at Mrs. Jeffries. "Mrs. Goodge is in the kitchen."

"He was speaking to me," said an unfamiliar, faintly accented voice. A tall, dignified, elegantly dressed gray-haired woman stood in the doorway of the room. "And most rudely, too."

"Madame Ramanova," Witherspoon cried in surprise. "What are you doing here?"

"I came to see why you missed your dancing lesson last night," she explained. "I was most concerned. If you continue to miss lessons you'll never be ready for that ball next month."

"Dancing lessons?" Betsy repeated because she was terribly confused.

"Inspector Witherspoon has been taking lessons from me for the last week. We started last Friday evening. He's doing quite well," she said, nodding approvingly at her blushing pupil. "Why, at his Monday lesson he didn't step on my foot at all."

"You were taking dancing lessons on the nights of the murders?" Mrs. Jeffries couldn't believe her ears. Why hadn't he just told them where he was?

"Well, er, yes," Witherspoon admitted.

"Gracious, sir, why didn't you tell us? What time were you there?"

"Murder?" Madame Ramanova asked. "What murder?"

"From six till almost eight-thirty."

"So you had a bonafide alibi," Mrs. Jeffries exclaimed.

"I was embarrassed," the inspector explained. "I didn't want anyone to know that I didn't know how to dance properly."

"But sir, your life and liberty were at stake."

"Life and liberty," Madame Ramanova repeated. "What are you saying?"

"Oh, I was going to say something," Witherspoon said earnestly. "But only if Nivens arrested me."

"Arrested you!" Madame Ramanova began backing out of the room. "Excuse me, I think perhaps I'd better go."

"I'll see you tomorrow evening then," Witherspoon called.

"I'm sorry, but I'm afraid my class is full," said the dancing teacher as she ran for the front hall.

"But I'm a private pupil."

"I'll send you a refund." The front door slammed.

"But, but . . . oh dear," said Witherspoon as he looked helplessly at Betsy and Mrs. Jeffries. "Did you get the impression Madame Ramanova was rejecting me as a student?"

"Yes, sir, I'm afraid I rather did," Mrs. Jeffries admitted.

Betsy nodded. "I think the words 'murder' and 'arrest' put her right off you."

"But that's not fair. She's my dancing teacher. She must give me lessons. If she doesn't, how will I ever learn to dance in time to take Lady Cannonberry to that April ball?"